FIRE
HAZARD

by
Jessica Laurie

Independently Published by: Jessica Laurie

Sherbrooke, Québec, Canada

CREDITS

Editor: *Journey Bardati*

Chapter 1

I stand in the middle of the corridor in my house, by the stairs to the upper floor, flames ablaze all around me. I am trapped. Panic fills my chest. I spin, frantically looking for a way out. Then I hear her voice. Somewhere within this inferno, Caitlin is in danger.

"Sam!"

If I wasn't alert before, I am now. I have to find her. I have to save her.

"Sam! Help me!"

I psych myself up to run through the flames, willing to risk getting burnt. I rush to every room, but the doors are locked everywhere. I try to ignore the stinging in my lungs. I'm still alive, and my friend still needs my help. The ceiling above me creaks and whines. I barely manage to jump out of the way as charred drywall falls inches away from me.

"Caitlin!" I cough.

"Sam! Hurry!"

My panic rises along with the flames. I scream. The sound morphs into something like an alarm clock.

I wake up startled and punch the button that silences my alarm. I sit up in my bed and rub my face. Shaking my head, I sigh knowing my nightmare was more like a reflection of my reality. Another day. At least I get out of bed feeling good about the fact that I have the house to myself again. Mom has been taking longer shifts lately, which means she leaves early in the morning and gets back late. I look at myself in the mirror. My feathery, light brown hair points in different directions. I brush it out hoping I don't create too much static. I dress, as simply as ever, and head downstairs. Breakfast is usually just a fruit for me, I don't have much of an appetite in the morning. I put on my black converse, tearing open in several places, and the laces weren't always brown. I shoulder my backpack, packed with my lunch and schoolwork, and head out the door.

I leave the house mentally double checking that I packed my asthma pump and bottle of anxiety pills. Forgetting those would be like leaving my lungs at home — and I have gym today. My mom would also kill me if she found I forgot my pills at home again. She's already annoyed about having to spend her money on my medication. Finding that I'd forgotten them at home would prove that she's wasting her money on meds that I don't use — which I do, but there's no trying to reason with her. I grab my bike off the front lawn. I probably shouldn't leave it out in the open, but I use it so often it would be a pain to do anything other than drop it in the grass when I get home, and if it annoys Mom then it's just a little more worth it. I sail into the street, leaving my small, old-looking red house behind. The paint on the porch is peeling, the windows are covered in dust, and the front door is splattered in dirt, but it's not really that old, it just doesn't receive much maintenance. My mom doesn't really care about that kind of stuff. When she's not working, she usually just locks herself in her room or lounges around the living room getting high.

I pedal down the avenue, taking my usual five-minute route to school. My neighbourhood, in Edmonton, is a small maze of streets, connecting in some places, and in others stopping in dead ends. It's kind of nice living so close to school, especially since it means I live ten minutes away from Caitlin, who also happens to live five minutes from school in the other direction. The school is like the halfway point to each others' houses. The houses leisurely glide past my vision as I ride down the street. Most of them have a single floor, not including the basement. Some, like mine, are fortunate to have two— my dad's choice. All in all, a very average-looking neighbourhood.

I pass the rectangular sign that stands up on the school's front lawn, the name of the school almost hidden by an upgrowth of shrubs just beneath it, but the words Southwest Edmonton Regional High School are still visible. I swerve off one street onto the next avenue and into the parking lot accommodating a large bike rack station. Caitlin waits for me at one of the racks near a school entrance. She is wearing one of her geeky t-shirts today. I recognize it from the bit I can see out of the top of her hoodie. Her blonde hair, naturally shiny and smooth as usual, falls over her shoulders, neatly out of the way of her school bag, covered in buttons, pins, and key chains.

"Hey," Caitlin says.

"Hey," I push my ride into the rack and hang my helmet on the handles. Caitlin and I walk towards the entrance. Within a loose border of trees and shrubs lies our school, a large beige building.

"How're you doing?" asks Caitlin.

"Okay, but I had another claustrophobia attack last night." Caitlin's eyes soften, her brows furrowing, which I know means she cares but also kind of makes me feel more pitiful.

"Sam...did your mom corner you again?"

"Yeah," I answer.

Caitlin sighs. "Hey, three more years and you're out of there."

Three years. Graduation will mean I'll be of age to move out. That sounds like the light at the end of the tunnel I need, but it still seems so far away, like I can't get past this slow trudge through the mud that is my life right now.

We enter the school. The building holds an impressive number of workshops, labs, and studios, but almost everything about it is beige. Caitlin and I pass underneath the glass sign over one of the main passageways which welcomes students to Home of the Titans. We turn instinctively into the doorway of our first class of the day.

Science — one of my favourite subjects. It's one of the only things that helps me understand the world. Taking it apart bit by bit and learning how each piece functions gives me a sense of comfort, because fact seems to offer some kind of certainty. It won't change, it's not going anywhere.

A paper finds its place in front of me. "Congratulations again, Sam," says Miss Hicks.

Caitlin looks at me from across the isle of desks. She leans over and whispers. "What did you get?"

"Ninety-six. You?" Caitlin holds up her test. A seventy-eight.

"That's pretty good," I shrug.

Caitlin rolls her eyes jokingly. "Okay, Miss Nineties."

I smile. Caitlin is so smart. I'm school smart, but she seems to know a little bit of everything. Random facts. And she's always reading.

"Page 214, guys," Miss Hicks' voice projects from the front. I turn the pages of my heavy textbook and I finally flip to a diagram of the earth, its layers taken apart to show its different components. The crust, the upper mantle, the mantle, the outer core, inner core. Arrows jut out from each part indicating either their solid or liquid properties and the measurements of depth of each layer. The next page is laid out in blocks of factual texts on petrology. I flip another page for a hint of what's up next. More paragraphs describing geological phenomenon. I settle in for a fascinating discussion.

About an hour later, the classroom is filled with the sound of fluttering paper as notebooks are slapped shut and stacked on top of textbooks. Miss Hicks' final comments are drowned out as students stand and push in their chairs. My second class, art, is my favourite of the two electives I chose for this year, the other being chemistry. Caitlin, having choses film studies and baking, meets up with Wallace, whom she calls her "baking buddy." Their talk of soufflé fades behind me as we wave to each other on our way out of the classroom.

In the art room, Justine and Joey are already sitting, early as always. How they get from one place to another so quickly always amazes me. Throughout the room, tall chair stools sit tucked underneath black glossy tables which come higher off the ground to allow students to work standing if the project demands it. I take a seat across from Justine and Joey at our usual spot at one of the tables near the center of the room.

"Hey guys," I say.

"Good morning," says Justine.

"Babe, did I bring my clementine, or did I leave it in my locker?" Joey looks around in confusion. Justine and Joey have been dating for two years. Sometimes I wonder at the fact that they are still together because I've never imagined that high school relationships ever last very long... Maybe that's why I've never bothered with a boyfriend. Still, I've known them for almost as long as they've been dating and they seem to be maintaining their relationship very well.

"I don't know!" Justine laughs, "I'm not the guardian of your snacks."

"Ugh," Joey groans, "I'm hungry."

"Well, lunch is right after this class. You'll survive."

"I guess."

Their dialogue is cut off by Mrs. Rodriguez. The art

5

teacher waits for everyone to turn their attention to the front. She wears a colourful button up shirt patterned with what looks like a mix between flowers and patches of paint. Her top is paired with beige pants, as if she wanted her bottom half to camouflage into the school walls.

"I'll be quick. As I mentioned last week, today we will be continuing our projects. You should be just about done. Thursday will be your last chance to finish up any detail and then you'll be handing them in at the end of class. Any questions?" Mrs. Rodriguez's eyes scan the room. When no one says anything, she adds, "Well, with that I'll let you get on with your paintings. Happy art-ing."

That's like her slogan. Justine and I give each other smirking glances at this. The students who hadn't gotten their canvases from the display counter get up now, including me. I take the tabletop easel to my seat and roll up my sleeves. My arms exhibit a few bruises, which don't look too abnormal, so I'm not concerned with people seeing them. I look at my canvas. I tried to implement the glazing technique we learned, meant to create a sort of faded effect. My painting shows a dove flying out of a broken cage hanging in an open window. I am always very critical of my art, and even after working on it for the sum of about a week I still doubt its quality.

Justine nods towards my painting. "How's your project coming along?"

"I'm not sure..." I sigh.

Justine gets up and walks around the table to look at my artwork. Her head tilts as she examines it. "I like the symbolism. Breaking free." Justine loves symbolism. It must be one of her favourite aspects of art. And she often plays with juxtapositions of life and death. Once, she had shown me her own project— a flower bed against a metal fence, half of the flowers withering, the other half blooming. She said it was meant to reflect society. How, below the surface, our roots are all interconnected but

6

the strong thrive alongside the weak without sharing their supplies. Something deep like that.

"Thanks," I say.

"I just hope it doesn't come from actual feelings of entrapment" she jokes. I laugh for her sake.

"Don't worry," I lie. "I just like the imagery."

I look up at Joey, who looks despairingly at his own painting. Joey is more into hands-on mediums like clay and plaster, which is what we're moving onto after Christmas break.

"At least your imagery looks like something nice," Joey chuckles, looking incredulously at his own work. "Mine looks like a pile of shit married a skunk's ass." I try to suppress my laughter, but it comes out as a snort. Justine rolls her eyes and smiles at her boyfriend's notorious melodrama.

"That's definitely quite the imagery," Justine says. Joey leans his face onto his fist and plops his paintbrush in the colour green. "I can't wait for January..." he sighs.

It's September, and the weather is perfect. I would happily wear jeans and a light hoodie all year round if I could. Although everything is slowly dying, the cool and fresh air rustles through the changing leaves, splashing more colour into my surroundings. The grass, mostly green, stretches under the sun, still shining proudly in the sky. In the locker room, I slip on my loose shorts and get ready to enjoy one of our last weeks of gym outside. I pop my asthma pump into my pocket and follow Caitlin to the jogging track. My other thirty-some classmates jog on ahead of Caitlin and I. She always stays behind with me. The gym teacher, a short and stout blonde woman, stands on the side lines and watches. A kid, Lucas, I think, has already finished his first lap. Past the finish line, he drags his feet, sweating profusely and clutching his stomach. Our teacher yells at him.

"Lucas! Did you have a big lunch again today? You knew we were running."

I chuckle. Caitlin looks over at me.

"What's funny?"

I shake my head. "Lucas."

Caitlin turns her head and to see Lucas looking like he's about to puke. "Oh, Lucas," Caitlin sighs. "Hey, remember that kid in grade three?"

"Wow," I laugh. "That really narrows it down."

"Sorry. I just thought about that thing that happened during our big math test, with the glue."

"Oh, yeah! What was his name?"

"Maverick."

"Maverick!" I grin. "That name suits him, it sounds mischievous."

"It does!"

"So, Maverick brought crazy glue to class —" I remember.

"And he put some all over Mrs. Jane's chair before she entered the class. She sat on the glue for the whole test, so when she stood up finally —" Caitlin's giggling makes it harder to contain my own laughter.

"The back of her pants stayed glued to the chair." Caitlin and I look at each other, then we both burst into laughter.

"We shouldn't be laughing, poor Mrs. Jane."

"Yeah, but it was so funny!" says Caitlin. My laughter breaks into coughing which then turns to choking. Caitlin eyes me and slows her pace.

"Do you need to stop?" Caitlin asks me. I nod, annoyed, and stop to take my asthma pump out of my shorts pocket. I inhale while one of the sporty guys in the class gives me a demeaning glance as he jogs by confidently.

"Idiot," Caitlin says under her breath. "That guy always gloats over anyone who isn't athletic like him, I hate it."

"It's okay, Cait," I inhale.

"No, it's not okay for him to treat you like that," she argues. I shrug, which makes her laugh. "Nothing shakes you does it?" I manage a chuckle. Caitlin looks out to the rest of our class moving forward as she waits for me to recover. My smile quickly fades.

In the locker room, I pack my things slowly, deep in thought. Yesterday I had Careers class, which fed a lingering and growing concern. Girls on either side of us file past our isle towards to door. Caitlin catches the concerned look on my face.

"Sam, what's up?" I try to piece the words together in my head. Finally, I look at my friend.

"I was just thinking about what you said earlier. About nothing shaking me."

"Okay." She pauses. I struggle to untangle my thoughts, and I realize Caitlin is still waiting for me to follow up. A nervous laughter escapes my mouth.

"I don't know."

"Sam?" she presses. I sigh and look at her in the eyes.

"It's just, at this point, lots of our classmates are starting to figure out what they want to do in life. And you've known since you were, what, ten? And I still have no idea."

"You still have time. Sam, you have three years to figure it out," Caitlin reasons.

"Yeah, but what if I don't choose right?" And it spills out, my fatal flaw now finds itself on display after so many debates and wrestling sessions with myself. "How do I know that I'll be good at what I pick? If I become a scientist, would I be able to contribute to the advancement of the field by creating something that will benefit the world as much as other scientists in the past? If I become an artist, how do I know that my art can impact people the way I want it to? If I'm a teacher, not only do I have to

9

teach effectively, but I also have the pressure of knowing that I'm responsible for encouraging the next generation to contribute to the world in their own future careers. How do I know that I can fill that kind of role?"

"You're overthinking it."

"Okay, well, how did you know you wanted to be a veterinarian?"

"It's simple. I love animals, and I know I want to be the one to keep them healthy. If I overthought it, I could definitely find ways to fill my mind with insecurities and doubts about my abilities, but then I wouldn't know if I never tried. All I know is that this is what I want to do and I'll see how things go from there." Once again, I find myself jealous of my best friend. She has a good family that loves her, a home she feels safe in, and she knows exactly where she's going. And once again I start to feel small, like I have absolutely no control over my future. Caitlin swings her bag over her shoulder.

"You're super smart, Sam. And you have lots of talents. You'll figure it out. I know you will. Now come on, we'll be late for History."

I sit in History class, adding doodles to my already doodle-full notebook, and think about how much I want to go home, or at least not be at school. It's my final class of the day. I fidget with the pendant on my necklace, basically the only piece of jewelry I own, and one that I like. It's a little red flower with glossy petals at the end of a sliver chain. My father gave it to me before he left, and it's the only thing he ever gave me that holds meaning. Hearing my name, I am jolted out of my thoughts. I raise my head.

"When did Canadian soldiers assail Juno Beach?" the teacher asks me. I risk a glance around the classroom, expecting some judging eyes, but mostly I just see that I'm not the only one looking forward to the end of the day.

Caitlin sticks her tongue out the side of her mouth from across the classroom. I try not to smile.

"June sixth, nineteen forty-four," I respond dully. The teacher gives me a stern look and then leaves me alone. Thankfully, the bell rings, and my school day is over. I let myself be carried out into the hallway with the current of students.

"Sam! Wait up!" Caitlin says as she catches up with me.

"Oh, sorry," I say.

"You really looked like you were waiting for that bell to ring," she comments.

"I was."

Caitlin looks thoughtful for a moment. "I know!" she says perkily. "Let's race to my place." I smirk. She raises her eyebrows and then speeds off.

"Hey!" I hurry after her.

Caitlin and I speed down the street and turn a corner. Caitlin darts ahead of me, a large smile on her face. I have an idea. I know these streets well. I hug a corner to my right and disappear into a new street. I pedal as hard as I can without exhausting my strength, following the bend of the cul-de-sac. I emerge on the other end, right in front of Caitlin, whose face I am delighted to see exhibits a look of surprise.

"Oh no you don't!" Caitlin cries from behind me. I laugh maliciously. I quickly glance back and see Caitlin is already closer behind. We turn another corner and I have to swerve to avoid an oncoming car.

"Careful!" Caitlin calls. Caitlin has caught up now and is quickly closing in. I slow down, beginning to feel the air leave my lungs. Caitlin screeches to a halt in front of her lawn. I arrive a moment later.

"You cheated," I huff.

"How did I cheat!?"

"You allowed yourself a head start. Besides, I have asthma."

"Oh, okay. Can you just admit that I won?"

"Whatever."

Caitlin and I barge through her front door, red in the face from our race. She has a cute blue family home, with garage and everything. Caitlin empties her school bag onto the kitchen table and sighs.

"Miss Dung assigned us half the book to read for next week, like we don't have anything else to do for school." A laugh slips out of my throat.

"Miss Dung? Is that what you guys call Miss Dunt?"

"Yeah, she's a crap teacher. By the way, you want to stay for supper?"

"If it's okay with your mom."

"Dude, you've been coming over since Pre-K. Anyway, if we're done homework before supper maybe we could watch a movie? I've got Twizzlers."

"That is tempting. It can't be too long though, I have to be home by nine."

Caitlin furrows her brow. "You're not twelve anymore."

"Yeah, well, tell that to my mom." Mrs. Moore, Caitlin's mom, walks into the kitchen, rocking skinny jeans, a white blouse, and a grey cardigan. Mrs. Moore is a cool mom, and always dresses really fashionably, which I admire. The extent of my wardrobe pretty much ends at jeans and t-shirts.

"Hi, Sam. Staying for supper again this evening?"

"Yeah, if that's okay." Mrs. Moore smiles at me and I feel dumb for saying that like I always do.

"You know you're always welcome," Mrs. Moore says warmly. I perceive Caitlin's raised eyebrows in the corner of my eye.

"I told you," Caitlin mouths. Mrs. Moore grabs an apple from the fruit bowl on the counter and turns.

"Well, gotta get back to my desk. I only have a few more hours of work."

"Have fun," Caitlin calls as her mom leaves the room. Mrs. Moore winks at her daughter. Caitlin's mom is a developer, building reports for the company I always forget the name of. World something. I find it cool for Caitlin that she gets to have her mom around the house like that. We sort through our homework and work on it for all of thirty minutes before we inevitably get distracted. Now we are both slumped in our chairs, scrolling through social media.

"He's so cute!" Caitlin exclaims suddenly. I wonder if she's talking about the new Spiderman again. She had dragged me into the theatre as soon the newest movie had come out this past summer. Now she's obsessively waiting for any announcements about the upcoming sequel. I look up curiously. Caitlin turns her phone and I see that she's messing with me. 'He' is an adorable dog. I sigh lightheartedly. I know she finds herself very comical. "For real, though. Why don't we ever talk about boys like regular teenage girls?" she adds.

"Maybe it's because none of the boys at school are really that interesting."

"Not true! Noah is really funny. Every time I see him in the hall with his friends, he's always doing something fun or goofy," Caitlin insists. I raise a quizzical eyebrow. Caitlin rolls her eyes. "I don't like him, I'm just trying to make the point that there are interesting guys around, you just never bother to notice."

We have eggplant parmesan for supper. One of Caitlin and Mrs. Moore's favourite vegetarian dishes. Mr. Moore came home about an hour before we all sat down at the table. Mr. Moore is a university professor, teaching ancient Greek history. I've passed by his home office down the hall. The walls in there are covered in bookshelves, more stacks of books piled on his desk, and baskets overflowing with papers. Mrs. Moore is the organized one. Her office is almost the complete opposite of her husband's, with neatly placed office supplies and a few books on C++ and calculus. A bookshelf holds her personal collection of novels, fictions like Jane Austen and Charles Dickens.

"How was your day, Cait?" Mr. Moore asks.

"Good. I brought home the soufflé I made today," says Caitlin.

"Desert!"

Both of Caitlin's parents are pretty fit people. They have a treadmill, a yoga ball, and sets of weights in the basement which Caitlin is still trying to motivate herself to use. Mr. Moore lifts a spoonful of eggplant to his mouth. "So what do you girls have planned for tonight?"

"A movie," Caitlin scoops food onto her fork. "Don't know which one yet." She glances at me. "And Twizzlers."

I nod in agreement.

"Sounds like fun," says Mr. Moore.

The sound of water draining from the kitchen sink finally ceases as Mr. Moore finishes the dishes. Caitlin stands in front of their movie shelf in the living room.

"What are you in the mood for?"

I sit on the couch and work at opening a pack of Twizzlers. I'm not super picky when it comes to movies, and I know she's kind of a geek so I'll just go along with whatever. The layout of the Moores' home is similar to mine except a bit bigger, and way nicer. Their living room is cozy, laid out with a brown couch, a burgundy sofa chair, and an oval-shaped coffee table sitting on top of a white rug. I've never understood that — how can you keep a white rug clean?

"Mmm, action?"

"Would you also be up for Sci-Fi?" I finally get the pack of Twizzlers open. Caitlin spins around to look at me with mock offence. "You're gonna start eating them without me?" I pop a Twizzler into my mouth.

"No."

Caitlin laughs and shakes her head. She turns back to face the shelf, grabs a movie and twists around again, holding up a DVD.

"Hitch Hiker's Guide to the Galaxy?"

"Sure," I shrug. Caitlin places the disk in the DVD player and plops down next to me. She sticks her hand in the Twizzler bag and pulls one out so fast it breaks in half. We giggle. She sticks her hand deeper into the Twizzlers for her missing piece which comes out as a quarter piece. We giggle harder.

"Okay," she says decisively and tears the Twizzler bag open. "There." I peel another one out. I didn't know how many I expected to eat. I didn't know what time we started the movie, and that was my mistake.

I practically jump off my bike when I roll onto the front yard. It's ten o-clock, and my heart is pounding. It's not that I care about what my mom thinks, I just care about what she might do. I unlock the front door and open it very slowly, hoping to God she's already asleep. I close the door very gently behind me and lower my bag quietly onto the floor.

"Where've you been?" says my mom from the living room, too loudly for this time of night. I jump and look over to where she sits slumped on the couch, an empty heroine syringe on the coffee table. Great.

"I was at a friend's house. Our movie ended later than we thought." Amy stands up. She approaches me, her eyes dark with danger.

"Oh! You have friends now, huh?" she mocks. I

force myself not to shout. When she makes comments like that it makes me mad not because they're mean but because they're just so stupid, like she enjoys getting her insults from an elementary schoolyard. I roll my eyes instead, to show her my annoyance.

"I'm going to bed." I start towards the stairs but she hurries over and grabs my arm.

"Hey! You're not going anywhere. You can't just march into my house, after your curfew, and think that it's all good."

"I'm sorry, okay. It won't happen again," I say in an attempt to appease her.

"Sorry," she huffs. "Sorry won't cut it, hon. I've had a shitty day, I don't need to come home and deal with my slutty daughter who goes out till late at night doing who knows what —" I pull my arm away. She tries to throw whatever insult she can at me when she's in this state, even if she knows Caitlin is my only friend and there is nowhere else I really go besides her house.

"I don't know what else to say. And I'm sorry you had a shitty day, but that's not my fault," I say impatiently. My cheek bursts into a burning sensation as Amy's hand collides with my face. I recoil from the impact.

"I'm sorry," Amy mocks. "Bullshit!" The stinging still lingers on my skin when Amy slaps me again, harder this time. I fall to the floor. My eyes water from the pain. I blink. "You're not sorry. You only care about yourself, and your perfect little grades, and your stupid little friend."

"Sorry," I choke out a laugh. "I don't have stupid friends." Amy's face hardens, and I flinch, expecting to be rewarded with another blow.

"You are just like your father. Careless, ignorant, good-for-nothing."

"Yeah? Well, that's already better off than you!"

16

At this point I don't care what she does, her attitude is the worst thing I deal with from her every day anyway because it guarantees a negative outlook on everything, no matter what I do or say. It means we can never have a proper conversation. The underneath of her foot makes contact with my stomach. I fold.

"I'm going to bed. I don't want to see your face." Good, I don't want to see yours. Amy shuffles up the stairs to her room, which is unfortunately across the hall from mine. I am left here on the floor, my stomach and face aching. I take in a shaky breath. Then I exhale glumly when I remember it's only Tuesday. A new day is all I can hope for when I live with her. And every morning is a day closer to when I no longer have to.

Chapter 2

I wake up with a headache, my face buried in my pillow. I take my time getting out of bed — I don't bother rushing because it only really takes me about fifteen minutes to get ready in the morning. I wash cold water over my face, the slap marks having faded overnight. I smooth out my hair and get ready to head out. I don't eat, but throw a snack into my backpack and make sure all my homework is in order, then I'm out the door.

As I pedal down the street, a little girl passes by me on her little bike. I remember when I first learned to ride a bike. I was five. My dad taught me on this very street, before he left. I remember him holding onto the back of my seat and telling me that I was capable of anything. That's just what I needed to hear in my nervousness. He let go and I squeaked. But as I rolled down the street, my swerving became striding.

"Look at her go!" he called out. "She's on fire!" That put a smile on my face. I did it, I achieved something, and someone was proud of me. I laughed and biked on with more confidence.

My first class flies by in a blur, partly due to the headache. Also, I never have a mind for math in the morning, and now regret not having thought about taking a Tylenol or something before leaving the house. I had checked my bag when I got to school, even though I was certain there was nothing for my headache there. I half-consciously hand in my assignment when the bell rings. I make my way out of the classroom, feeling the energy of the others students bouncing off me in the halls, but none of them share. I adjust my posture and try not to drag my feet for my own sake. Wake up, Sam. This isn't the first time your morning starts this way. Somehow you never quite get used to it — I wonder how many other students secretly go through this kind of stuff at home. How could I know anyway? Who wants to share that misery?

Recess is one of my favourite parts of the school day. Especially at this time of year when I can enjoy some cool, fresh air, something I really need today. In the midst of campus there are two outdoor courtyards, nice green patches meant for lounging outdoors, but Caitlin and I like to hang out at the park that lies just behind the school building. It's a wide space speckled with soccer nets and trees and allows us to sit somewhere a little more secluded. Today, Caitlin and I sit under our favourite tree. It's not very big — not forest big — but it's a nice spot. Somewhere on the bark we had carved our initials: S+C=BFFs. It's cheesy but we don't care. Caitlin taps on her phone, I draw.

"Did you know centaurs have two rib cages?" Caitlin says without looking up from her phone.

"You're such a nerd," I laugh.

"Me? You're one to talk, Miss I'm-super-good-at-science." I jokingly roll my eyes at her. "Well, which one contains the lungs?" I ask reluctantly.

"The human ribs!"

"How do you even know this? From a book?"

"No, I looked it up. Wanna see a picture?"

"I'll pass. Honestly sounds kind of gross." Caitlin ignores me and shoves her phone into my line of vision, forcing me to look at centaur anatomy. I turn my head away. "That's really disturbing."

Caitlin pulls her phone away. "I think it's cool."

"You're weird." Caitlin raises her eyebrows. "In a good way," I reassure. I go back to drawing nothing in particular.

"By the way, we still hanging out this weekend?" Caitlin and I hang out most weekends, but for some reason we always feel the need to make it a plan.

"Yeah!"

"What do you have in mind?" she asks.

I wanted to say, 'after the night I had I would be glad to get out of the house for almost any reason,' but I wouldn't want to make her feel bad. "Anything," I say. "And lots of Twizzlers." Caitlin smiles, oblivious.

I drone through the rest of the day. My English teacher's voice buzzes in the air as she reads excerpts of our book out loud, and I try to be more alert in chemistry because none of my other classes carry a risk of explosions. In Careers, my mind flies off somewhere distant. I am only briefly aware of a new assignment coming up requiring us to outline our top three career choices. The final bell rings and students flood out of the front doors. Caitlin and I grab our bikes and roll them to the sidewalk together.

"See you tomorrow!" Caitlin calls as she mounts her bike.

"See ya!" We head in opposite directions, homeward.

I see it almost immediately. I walk into the kitchen and glare at the lengthy list of chores taped to the fridge, sighing as I drop my homework-heavy bag on the floor. Stress begins to overwhelm me because I know I won't be able to get everything done — not all the chores, not all my homework, and that means penalty on both sides. I pick up my bag and rush into my room. Seated on my bed, I slip two anxiety pills into my mouth, then proceed to spend a large part of the late afternoon cleaning the bathrooms, vacuuming, dusting. I leave the dishes in the sink when I see how much time has passed — it's time for homework. I sit on the couch and inhale from my pump.

Taking a book out of my bag, I try not to panic when I see how many pages need to be read.

It's eight-thirty when my mom comes home. A bowl has been added to the pile of dishes from the mac and cheese I had for supper. She staggers through into the kitchen with a brown paper bag in her hand. She sees the dishes overflowing from the sink onto the counter. I try to keep my eyes on the book, knowing she will probably have a fit.

"You didn't do any of the chores," she spits. I drop my book onto the coffee table and get up from the couch. Maybe if I can get to my room she will leave me alone. Then I realize that's a stupid thought. "Uh-uh. Stay right there." I drop my hands to my sides in irritation and sigh. "I did some of them. I vacuumed and cleaned the bathrooms and stuff, but I have a lot of homework due for tomorrow and — "

"You have no respect. I work my ass off every day at that shitty little gas station to keep my ungrateful, lazy, bitch of a daughter fed. You don't understand my struggle. If only you had this shit in your system." She holds up the brown paper bag in her hand. "Maybe you'd understand and have more respect for your poor old mom."

"You don't know what you're saying. And that's the thing, I don't want to understand. You're psycho, and as soon as I graduate, you won't have to worry about your 'lazy, bitchy' daughter anymore, cause by then I'll be moving out, and you'll never have to see my face again." Amy furiously tears the bag open to reveal a syringe and begins to stomp towards me. I hurry towards the stairs to lock myself in my room, but Amy gets to me before I can make it. She grabs me by the back of my shirt and pulls me away from the stairs. She drags me into a corner and holds me there. This is the worst thing she could possibly do to me. As claustrophobia takes over, my limbs go weak, I begin to hyperventilate, my face twisting into an expression of panic. When my lungs stop taking in air, my brain begins to shut down, the corners of my vision darkening.

Using this to her advantage, Amy brings the syringe down on me. With what remains of my strength I grab her hands and try to push the syringe away. My arms tremble and finally give out. Amy stabs the syringe into my thigh. I yell and my body slips into shock. I feel my pupils dilate, my heart violently pumps the drug through my veins, into my system. I slide down to the floor as my body trembles out of control. Through blurred vision I see Amy rise, out of breath.

"Enjoy it while it lasts," Amy spits and leaves me to pass out.

Eight-year-old me stands in the entrance to the living room, trying to stay out of sight. My parents are fighting again. It's been a lot more often lately, and it scares me.

"You don't understand my struggle so why don't you shut up?" yells my mom.

"Cocaine isn't going to solve your problems, Amy. Is this the kind of environment you want for our daughter?" counters my dad. I've hear that word before — cocaine— I don't know what it is exactly but I know it's been the source of my mom's bad moods and the cause of my parents' fights.

"Oh! So we're in the same boat here? You know what it feels like to be depressed? Huh?" my mom hisses.

"Here we go again. Amy, how many times have I offered us a new life? A chance for us to have a fresh start back home? New York has so much more to offer than Edmonton. I get that you're in pain, but if you just gave this a chance, it could be good for you, help you rehabilitate."

"And what about my home? I'm just supposed

to leave everything I know here and follow your ass to America? I don't need your rehabilitation plan, James! I'm dealing with my life in my own way and if you have a problem with that than you can go back to your pretty little New York."

"Then marriage means nothing to you? Dealing with your life in your way... How are we supposed to raise a family if we're not on the same page?"

Amy throws her hands up and turns her back to him as if to say that this conversation is over. Sometime later, I am still in the living room entrance, but my dad is gone and my mom sits on the couch with her head buried in her hands. I walk towards her.

"Mommy? When is Daddy coming home?"

My mom's face remains hidden. "Daddy isn't coming back."

"Why?" I ask sadly.

"Because," Amy looks up at me. "Mommy is going through something, and Daddy is a selfish bastard."

"What's a bastard?"

"Never mind," my mom sighs. I stare at her, confused.

"He's never coming back?"

"No, Sam! He's not coming back, I just said that," she raises her voice. "It's over, you won't see Dad again." I begin to cry.

I wake up on the floor, right where Amy left me, head throbbing. Using the kitchen table for support, I slowly stand on wobbly limbs. I look at the time on the oven — It's ten a.m. I can feel anxiety kick in when I realize that I'm late for school. Still, my body is begging me not to rush. I drag my feet over to the kitchen sink to splash water over my face. I drink directly from the tap and lean over the sink for a moment, letting the water run uselessly, my eyes fixed on the tap. I have to make it through the day. I can't afford to get behind in my schoolwork. My grades are the only thing I have, my ticket out of here. Finally, I take a deep breath and turn off the water. In my day-old clothes, unbrushed teeth, and uncombed hair, I grab my bag and head out the door in a hurry. I bike through my stiffness and queasiness. Thank God it's only a five-minute bike ride.

I walk in through the school's front doors and immediately feel uneasy. The halls are vacant, the air is quiet. I try to walk quietly so I don't have to hear my footsteps echo. My heartbeat quickens with the dreadful thought that all eyes will be on me when I walk through the classroom door, half an hour later than I'm supposed to. When I step in, I realize I must look like a mess. I quickly brush my disheveled hair out of my face and pray that no one notices I am wearing the same outfit as yesterday. Miss Hicks stops mid-sentence to join her gaze with the other twenty-five. I keep my eyes fixed on my desk in an effort to ignore the awkward silence. Once I've sat down, Miss Hicks speaks.

"I'll see you after class, Sam." She resumes her teaching and I silently pull my books out of my bag, glancing over at Caitlin.

"What happened?" she whispers. I shake my head and turn my attention back to the front. I feel her eyes on me but try not to look at her again.

I pack up my things slowly and wait for everyone to shuffle out of the classroom. Caitlin points to the door, her eyes intent, and I know she means that she'll be waiting outside the classroom . I nod. I approach Miss Hicks, who sits at her desk writing on a slip of paper. She looks up. "You okay, Sam? You're never late to class."

"I overslept," I say, which is true, but I wouldn't tell her why.

"Are you sure that's all? You look kind of ill to me."

"I'm probably just coming down with a cold. I

won't be late again." I try to answer confidently but Miss Hicks still looks concerned.

"Okay," she says, trying to believe me. "Make sure you get some rest when you get home. I admire your dedication to your schoolwork, but sometimes it's also good to give yourself a break."

"Yeah. I will. Thanks." I turn to leave.

"And Sam." I face her again. She holds up the slip of paper she had been writing on earlier. "As much as I dislike doing this, you need to bring this late slip to the Main Office." I take the slip willingly. "See you next class."

"See ya," I say and walk out of the classroom holding the slip up for Caitlin to see. She gets off the wall she was leaning on. "I have to bring this to the Main Office." Caitlin's eyes widen.

"That's your first slip, like, ever. Why were you late?" Caitlin and I walk down the hall.

"I don't feel super great today."

"We have gym later, you gonna be okay?"

"Yeah, I'll push through it." Caitlin raises her eyebrows at me like I've said something unwise. She's probably right, but I don't want to feel like anything is wrong. If it wasn't for my mother's absurdity, this would just be another regular school day — and I really want it to be.

I barely touch my painting in art class. It's our last chance to finish up our projects and I feel no motivation whatsoever. Justine notices.

"Your painting looks great, Sam. Just add a little more shading by the window and it should be good to hand it."

"It's not that," I sigh. Justine examines me.

"Coming down with something?"

"Feels like it, yeah."

"Flu season is coming up, maybe you caught it early," Joey suggests. "In which case, keep your distance, I don't want you to infect me before my soccer game this weekend." Justine slaps his arm.

"Joey!" Justine looks at me. "He's just kidding. For real though, you should get some water. It'll probably help."

"Yeah, I think I'll do that." I push my chair back and grab the hall pass.

I almost startle myself when I catch a glimpse of my reflection in the mirror. I look pale, sickly, and a little thin. What kind of drug did Amy bring home for me? I decide it's probably heroine and my body is just rejecting it since it's not something I'm used to ingesting. Then again, I don't know anything about what it's like to actually take drugs, I've just seen what it does to my mom.

I join up with Caitlin for lunch at the park. I can barely stomach my food. Caitlin's eyes move back and forth between me and my lunch.

"You're not eating?" she asks.

"I'm trying to."

"What is it? A cold? The flu?"

"I don't know yet, I just don't feel hungry."

"What did you have for breakfast?"

"Nothing."

"Sam! You can't eat nothing, especially if we're running in half an hour."

"I know," I say miserably. I stare down at my sandwich, then force myself to take a bite. I ignore my urge to gag, and swallow.

Caitlin and I head to the girl's locker room, making our way through the halls filled with anxious energy of friends making weekend plans or looking forward to sleeping in. Ten minutes later, when Caitlin ties her hair into a ponytail, about ready to make her way to the jogging track, I still lean over, tying my shoes.
Caitlin puts her hands on her hips. "Sam."

"It's okay, Caitlin. I'll meet you out there." Caitlin doesn't look happy that I'm pushing myself when I clearly look as ill as I feel. I avoid her eyes and she leaves. I am the only one left in the locker room. I stand slowly and clutch my stomach. I run to the toilets as soon as I feel myself gag. I vomit whatever bit of food I've had today. I take a couple of deep breaths, rinse my face and head out to the jogging track.

I join the rest of the group. When Caitlin sees me her eyes widen. I pretend not to notice. Then I'm aware that I'm shaking and sweating. When I reach Caitlin the teacher has already signaled us to start running. Caitlin and I jog side by side.

"You look worse than when I left you eight minutes ago. You sure you still want to jog today?"

"No," I admit. "I feel like I'm overheating."

"Yeah, you're shaking too. You should really sit out this time." I don't wait for her to say it twice.

"Sounds good." I turn around and make my way to the teacher. Caitlin looks back at me as I sit on the benches. I watch her run on her own. She is jogging faster than usual, and I try to push away the thought that I'm dead weight to her. I know she cares about me, I just always assume the worst of people, I guess. I hug my knees and close my eyes. I feel a hand on my shoulder and look up. My teacher, her blonde hair tied back into a ponytail like always, stands beside me.

"Sam, you look like you need to go home and rest. I just called the Main Office. You're good to go home early today." I nod my head silently, get up from the bench and walk towards the school building.

I get home early, thankful for some extra time to rest, but another list of chores laughs at me from the fridge. I tear it off the door and, to my chagrin, it unfolds to twice its length. My eyes skim the page, spotting all the chores

I just did yesterday on top of a ton of new chores, many of them needless. I think of the schoolwork I wasn't able to do last night, the embarrassment I felt this morning as the entire class stared at me, the way I've been feeling horrible all day — all because of her. I let out a cry of frustration — and the list bursts into flames. I scream and drop the list onto the floor. I look at my smoking hand in shock. The paper on the floor shrivels up and the last little flame fades.

I stand there dumbfounded, and then feel more astonishment wash over me when I discover I no longer feel terribly ill. I turn around speedily and grab a useless flyer from the stack of mail on the kitchen counter. I hold it in front of me and stare at it wide-eyed, my hand shaking. I wait a moment and then it, too, bursts into flames. I drop it into the sink and turn the tap open onto it. I swallow. Maybe I've finally gone mad. Maybe that drug Amy injected into me just threw me right over the edge. I'm totally hallucinating. I look at my open hand and concentrate. I need to prove to myself that I'm just imagining this. My palm produces a flame. My mouth opens in bafflement. I close my hand and the flame extinguishes. I open and close my hand in repetition and watch the flame come to life and die over and over. I stare at my fist. Whatever is happening to me, I need to know more, and there's no time to waste.

Chapter 3

I run upstairs to my room, ignoring the million chores I have to do. I hop onto my bed with my second-hand laptop. It's really old and slow, my mom managed to get it from a friend or something. I pull up the web and begin typing words like "real life superpowers," "superpower experiments," "superpower drug," and "fire powers" into the search bar. All I get are comic book references, superheroes — all fictional things. I try writing essentially the same thing in different ways, using various terms, but I just get the same results. I slap my laptop shut, discouraged. I can't help thinking that the one person I know who would be able to help me figure this out is Caitlin, but what would she think? We've known each other almost all our lives, but nothing like this has ever come up to test whether she would believe me insisting this kind of thing is real. I have a feeling she'd want to believe, being the superhero fanatic that she is. I could also ask Miss Hicks about the scientific aspect behind this phenomenon. I have confidence in her knowledge, and since I can't find anything online, maybe she would be able to offer some kind of useful information. My thoughts lead back to Caitlin. I want to tell her, but also... I'll let my tomorrow-self make that decision. I've had enough to worry about today, and who knows what this evening holds?

The bell rings for recess, students pour out into the halls. I go to Caitlin's locker and wait for her there.

"Hey," she says when she sees me. Caitlin opens her locker and swaps textbooks.

"Hey, I have to see a teacher about something, so I'll see you at lunch."

"Okay... Yeah. That's fine. See you at lunch," she says. As I leave I glance back to see a sort of apprehension on Caitlin's face. It only lasts a second but I notice. What was that about? I avert my eyes before she looks up again. I weave my way past students and turn into the doorway to Miss Hicks' classroom. I wait as she finishes answering a student's question. When the student passes by me as they leave, Miss Hicks waves at me.

"Hey Sam, come on in." I enter the classroom and walk over to her desk. "What's up?" she says. "Feeling better since yesterday?"

"Yeah, I am. Thanks." That's only half true. Physically, maybe, but very confused otherwise. "Um, I was wondering if you could answer a strange question." Miss Hicks tilts her head with interest. "Okay. How strange?"

"Has there ever been, in the history of science, an experiment that gave humans abilities?" Even as I'm saying it, I feel awkward and foolish. What kind of question is that? I imagine Miss Hicks thinks the same thing.

"Abilities?"

"I know this sounds weird, but like, for example, producing flames?" Gosh. I sound crazy. Why was this even a good idea? Miss Hicks chuckles, which makes me feel like even more of a child.

"I mean, science has allowed us to do incredible things but changing the biological design of human beings to the point of having abilities like producing fire or water is impossible... Are you wondering if powers are real?"

"No," I say a little too quickly. Suddenly I want to turn and leave. "I mean, that sounds crazy, I was just curious." What a lame answer.

"Is there a side project you're working on?" she asks.

"I guess it's kind of a project."

"Anything else I can help you with?" I know I should just leave it there, but I still have questions and I feel like she, the only teacher I really trust, might have answers. It's not only that she's my favourite teacher, that I enjoy her classes, or even because she teaches my favourite subject. She genuinely invests in her students, and I've always felt like she cares about me and my future. Her class is one of the only places where I can forget — for even a moment— what's going on with the rest of my life, so I push aside the voice whispering that this conversation is stupid.

"Yeah," I continue. "If, theoretically, it were possible that someone would gain the ability to, like, produce fire, how do you think that would be possible... theoretically?"

"Well..." she begins in a more serious tone. "If you take dragons for example, if they existed, they are theorized to have produced fire by bringing up a hydrogen and methane rich gas from their intestines and its contact with the oxygen in the air would create fire."

"And if it were to be produced through hands?" Now I've really thrown all reality out the window. Miss Hicks chuckles again.

"Hands? Well, this is definitely beginning to sound like a comic book." Her eyes drift to the side of her desk as she thinks. "I would say the gas would probably have to come from oil produced by the body, or maybe sweat? Did that answer your question?" She adds hesitantly.

"Yeah, I guess so. Thanks, Miss Hicks."

"May I ask what this project is about? I'm intrigued."

"It's a story I'm writing. About a girl who is exposed to chemicals that gives her the power to produce fire." Story of my life.

"That sounds interesting. I'd love to read it when you're done, if you don't mind." I smile. There's the teacher I love.

"Sure."

"If you have any more questions, don't be shy." I nod, and leave the classroom. Looking back, I feel like the conversation was kind of a waste of time and I could have spared the weirdness of it. What exactly was I expecting? That a science teacher would actually be able to help me figure out what I thought was impossible just yesterday? Honestly, what I need is someone who wants to believe that the impossible could be true and knows a plethora of fictional stories surrounding it.

Caitlin sits at one of the campus' picnic tables, eating lunch. Today she has a tofu salad, probably seasoned with one of her mom's homemade dressings she loves so much. Caitlin, along with her mom, is vegetarian. I've never thought to ask why, but at least for Caitlin I know it largely has something to do with her love for animals. I sit with my friend and take out a sandwich which I proceed to stare at instead of eat. My mind collects bits of my conversation with Miss Hicks. I begin to wonder if I will ever get real answers as to what is happening, and why it's happening. This can't be a coincidence, can it? Now, after all this time of life droning on in the same way as it always has, my mom suddenly decides that it's time I had a taste of what it's like to be on drugs? She wasn't exactly acting stranger than she usually does. Amy has always been selfish and greedy, she wouldn't waste her 'goods' on me, so why did she come home last night and decide whatever was in the syringe was meant for me? Nothing about that night makes sense, the more I think about it. And even if I asked her about it, why would she answer my questions, she's never —

"Sam?" Caitlin snaps me out of my thoughts. I look up at her large, questioning eyes. "How's the view up there? On the moon I mean?"

I shake my head. "Sorry."

Caitlin is looking at me intently. "What are you thinking about?"

I hope I didn't have too much of a troubled look on my face. I hesitate to spill it out. Whatever, how much weirder can things get, really?

"You believe in supernatural stuff, right?"

"Um. I mean, I like to think that angels watch over us, and I believe that ghosts could be real too. Although none of the ghost-hunting shows I've seen make it very convincing. They obviously set everything up — " Caitlin stops herself and looks at me more seriously as if she's just realized what I've asked her. "Why —"

"What about super-powers?" I spit out. Caitlin's eyes flutter and she shakes her head.

"What is this about?"

"You'd believe me if I told you something crazy right?"

"I guess it depends on how crazy it is. Sam, what's going on?" Caitlin squints now, as she does when she is trying to understand something.

"I think," I begin. "Something weird is happening to me."

"Are you being haunted? By a super ghost?" she says jokingly, but obviously still confused. I can't help but laugh at this.

"No. I don't know what's happening honestly, it's just —" I don't know how to continue from here. How do you go about telling someone that you have powers? "Never mind." I say finally. Maybe if I give up she'll forget about it, but even as I think this, I know I'm just fooling myself.

"Sam, you can tell me anything. 'Cause if you're being haunted by Gentleman Ghost or something, I'll totally stab him with nth metal for you." I know she's talking about something deeply geeky because I only manage to understand half of the sentence.

"Nth-what?"

Caitlin waves her hand dismissively. "Obscure DC reference. Ignore me." I laugh. Caitlin's superpower is bringing humour to any situation, it's one of the things I love about her. "Sam, what is it?" she urges me on. I can see that my stalling is starting to drive her crazy. I look her in the eyes honestly now.

"Promise you won't freak out?" As I say this I can see an earnestness fall over Caitlin's face like she's beginning to understand there's a real weight to this conversation.

"I won't."

"I think I might have some kind of ability?" It comes out as a question because saying it makes it feel real and I'm not really sure what 'real' is anymore.

"Like, what kind of ability?"

"Fire." I force the word out and try not to feel ridiculous. Caitlin sits still and stares, waiting for me to say more, but I don't.

"So, what are you saying? You can control fire?"

"No. I can, make it..." I cringe. This is harder than I thought.

Caitlin waves both hands in front of her. "Wait, wait, wait. Like, for real? How?"

Part of the tension in my chest releases. She believes me. Now I need to prove it. I look around briefly, making sure no one is close enough to see what I do next. I open my hand in front of me and a flame appears in my palm, flickering bright and warm. I watch Caitlin's eyes widen incredulously.

"How are you doing that?" she demands.

"I don't know. I just can." Caitlin is speechless. I can imagine her brain working behind her eyes, neurons pulsing as she tries to process this phenomenon.

"Okay, so this happened when?"

"Technically two days ago, and then the powers happened yesterday."

"What happened?" I must look uneasy because Caitlin's head tilts urgently like she knows it was something bad.

"Um, chemicals, I guess. It was this drug —"

"You did drugs?" Now I know she's overwhelmed because she knows I wouldn't go near that stuff.

"No, Caitlin. I didn't do drugs. They were forced on me."

"Wait, do you mean your mom?" I shrug. I've never actually told Caitlin that my mom is an addict. Her knowing about my mom's abusive nature is enough of a burden, it's a secret she's kept for me. Calling the police would mean being taken out of Amy's custody and being put into the foster system, since I have no other family — both my parents cut ties with their families, leaving them all behind them on a bad note. I convinced Caitlin that waiting until I'm legally allowed to move out wouldn't be the end of the world. She had been very sad and disturbed when I had told her, four years ago, but she had promised not to tell her parents. As difficult as it is, she respects me enough to keep this knowledge to herself. Now that I'm telling her about my ability, I have to tell her everything, otherwise anything else I tell her afterward would be a lie — and that's not how our friendship works. I proceed to tell her the facts: Why my dad left, my mom's switch to heroine, the paper bag, the syringe... I have never seen so much horror in Caitlin's eyes, and for a moment I feel bad for bringing this all down on her at once.

"Sam, that's really bad." She finally breaks through her shock. "She could get arrested for that."

"I know. I mean, there's still a chance that it might not be the drug, but it's the only logical explanation for what happened to me — if logic is even a thing now."

"You're right," Caitlin says determinately.

"This is crazy."

"You can't tell anyone, though, okay?"

"'Cause they'll kidnap and dissect you," she says as if quoting a familiar line.

"Honestly, maybe."

"I won't tell a soul."

"I knew I could count on you." I realize I had slowly leaned in throughout the conversation, as if to ensure secrecy, and I now lean back feeling good that Caitlin now knows everything. I look at my friend and I see a new expression spreading across her face. It's her idea face. She smiles and her eyes light up.

"What are you doing after school?"

I raise a questioning eyebrow.

Chapter 4

It's late afternoon, school ended less than an hour ago, and Mrs. Moore is out running errands. Caitlin has placed a row of standing logs in her backyard and paces in front of it with her hands clamped behind her back. I can already tell she's enjoying this. I stand a couple of meters away from her and wonder what exactly she expects me to do. She's set up in the middle of an open area, away from the garden, or any shrubs and trees, and especially — the back deck, her mother's safe haven. A fire extinguisher sits close by. Caitlin has tied her hair back into a ponytail and seems way more prepared than I am.

"With great power comes great responsibility," Caitlin quotes. That's a reference I do get — Caitlin and I watched that movie together.

"Cait, what are we doing?" I sigh. Caitlin stops in her tracks.

"You need to know how to use and control your powers. It's very important." She has taken on this character, perhaps feeling it suits our activity.

"And you would know this because you spend all of your free time reading comic books," I retort. Caitlin puts up a defensive index finger.

"That's not true! Lately I've been reading Percy Jackson." This just validates her geekiness. I make a face as if to say, "oh, of course." Caitlin moves on.

"First, we'll start big."
I frown. "How does starting big make sense?"

"Because it's easier to create bursts of energy than it is to concentrate that energy onto specific targets.

Now." She points to a log at the end of the line. "Show me how you throw fire." I let out a breath and shift uneasily, extremely uncomfortable with this whole idea. What if it all goes horribly wrong? What if, on top of everything, I find myself responsible for burning down the Moores' house?

I try a final protest. "Do I have to?" Caitlin just crosses her arms. "Fine."

I steady myself, fix my eyes on my target and then thrust my hand out towards it. Fire shoots out, and the log burns up instantly when my fire lands on it. Caitlin grabs the fire extinguisher and pulls the pin out with her teeth and spits it onto the grass. I raise my eyebrows, the hint of a smile tugging at the edge of my mouth. I can see that in her mind she is in her own sort of action film, so I hold back any comments. She sprays the log with the fluffy white foam.

"Easy. Now we need to see if you can control your fire in short bursts." She puts the fire extinguisher down then looks at me suddenly. "Can you run out of fire?"

I shrug. "I don't know."

"We'll find out soon enough." She turns and makes grand gestures as if to show off the row of logs that has been there from the start. "Okay, so now you're going to try to target each log, one after the other. In small bursts. Ready?" No. Not ready. But here we go anyway. I steady myself and then shoot one log after the other from left to right. I miss a couple of them, the fire landing in the grass instead. Caitlin extinguishes them. "Bursts are good. Gotta work on your aim a bit though."

"Work on my aim for what? What do you think I'll be doing with this? Superheroes aren't a real thing."

"Don't crush my dreams," Caitlin winks. "Let's try again."

The next thing I know it's nearing evening, and exhaustion has suddenly hit me. Feeling drained, I close my eyes for a second, and when I look up Caitlin has planted a stick into the ground.

"Final exercise. Now, try to concentrate your power out of a single finger and light the tip of the stick like a candle." I try to hold back a nervous laugh. After all the 'training' Caitlin has put me through this afternoon I feel none the more skilled or enlightened. Not that long ago I couldn't even hit all the logs with my fire balls and now she expects me to shoot fire out of a single finger? Yes, laugh-worthy indeed. Caitlin must see my hesitation. "You can do it," she says.

I try to concentrate and then point my index finger at the stick. Nothing happens. Now I know all my energy has run out. "It's not working."

"Maybe try a smaller quantity of fire through your palm." To please her I make a final attempt. I raise my palm towards the stick and push the air. The most pitiful bit of fire spits out of my hand, a cramp starts to form in my arm.

"What was that?" Caitlin laughs.

"Caitlin, I'm exhausted. We've been doing this for two hours." I see in her eyes that she feels bad now, realizing that she has pushed me to my limit.

"You're right. Sorry, I got carried away. It's just I've only dreamt of witnessing real powers like this."

"I get it." I swallow. "I think I need to go home now."

"Okay."

"See you tomorrow, Cait." I feel bad leaving so abruptly, with Caitlin standing looking dejected in the background. I hear her stacking the logs back into place as I leave through the wooden picket fence door and climb onto my bike. Mrs. Moore pulls into the driveway and waves at me as I leave their lawn. I put up a hand in return and pedal away. Was any of that worth it? All I can think right now is that the only advantage of practicing is to make sure I'm not out of control and cause something serious to happen. Suddenly I'm angry that I have to practice shooting fire at all. It's just another stress in my life. I never seem to get a break.

Jumping off my bike, I march over to the front door of my house, stomping through the entrance with a stack of mail in my hand, and toss them onto the small, scratched surface of the kitchen table. I drop my schoolbag on the floor with a thump and unzip it in a mildly aggressive manner to fish out my asthma pump and bottle of anxiety pills. I make the bottle about half empty by taking out two pills. I suck in some oxygen and stuff my medications into the pockets of my hoodie, then I turn to check out the mail. Mostly all junk, as usual. I throw the stack in the garbage bin, and that's when I see something that lights up the already existing spark of anger in me. A syringe. It's nothing I haven't seen before. Usually, Mom uses them in the privacy of her own room, but it's not uncommon for her to sprawl herself onto the living room couch, the syringe ending up in the kitchen trash. Tonight, I have zero tolerance. My anger flares and I raise my eyes with what I think, in the moment, is the greatest idea I've had in a while.

I open the door to my mother's room — a forbidden place. I search her things, carelessly tossing clothes and trash around. Finally, I open a drawer and find what I'm looking for. Her stash. Bundled up with socks and whatnot are the drugs that makes my mother's demons surface. I grab everything; the spoon, the syringes, the paper towels, the lighter, the powder, and throw the whole in her trash can. Despite my previous exhaustion, the anger has given me a new energy, and now my hand releases a wave of fire into the can. A malicious smile spreads across my face as I watch the contents burn and melt away.

I don't remember much after that, until I am woken up by the sound of my mom slamming the door to her room.

My eyes flutter open and I reach for my phone. It's nine p.m. Amy has just come home from her shift, in a bad mood again. My heart begins to beat faster when I remember what I did. In my blind anger I completely blotted out any consideration for consequence... and now I'm going to pay. I flinch as Amy slams her fist on the other side of my door.

"What did you do you brat!" Amy's voice yells.
I shuffle off my bed quickly and stand in middle of my room, eyes fixed on the door.

"I don't know what you're talking about."

"Open the door!" Amy is screaming now. "I swear that when I get my hands on you, oh, you'll regret stealing my stuff!" I brace myself for what happens next, my whole body tense with expectation. There is a moment of intensifying silence. Then I hear a scrambling noise and the doorknob trembles. It's one of those knobs easily unlocked from the outside with a coin, and I know that's what she's attempting now. I look around my room briefly wondering if there is anything I can defend myself with, but I barely have time to think about it before the door bursts open and the beast comes lumbering in. It all happens so fast. Amy's hands grip me and I am propelled backwards. My shoulders hit the wall. I am in a corner, unable to move. Panic begins to rise in my chest. On instinct I close my hands around Amy's forearms. She screams and stumbles away from me, looking down with a mixed expression of horror and confusion at the new hand-shaped burns that mark her skin.

"What the hell?" she says in a quieted voice. I look down at my hands which are now smoking. I can feel all the energy has come back to me. Earlier I had felt drained, it seems my unexpected nap provided a refill. "I'm calling the police." Amy turns out of the door. I reach out a hand to stop her.

"No!" Fire shoots out from my hand unintentionally and lands on the doorframe right beside Amy's head. My jaw drops. Amy's eyes widen with horror.

"You're a freak!"

"You made me this way!" I scream. "It was that crazy toxic drug you injected into me the other night!" We both ignore the flame licking its way up the doorframe. Amy backs away slowly.

"Don't you dare blame this on me! You're a bitchy good-for-nothing daughter. No one understands. That guy in the alley was the only one who seemed to have a clue how hard I work to keep this damn house standing, and that it isn't easy to deal with a kid who doesn't appreciate my efforts." Her voice is full of emotion. "I swear, he understood. He said, 'show her how you feel,' and I knew it was time you learned a lesson. I am not the bad guy."

My mind spins. "What!? Who are you even talking about? None of what you said made sense!" Despite all the animosity I have experienced from Amy, she has never been a liar. I've always known her to speak her mind and say exactly what she means. And that's what makes all of this even more confusing.

"And see, that's exactly why I would never take drugs willingly, because I would never want to become like you!" I throw my hands down in anger. Fire bursts out of my fists and the floor around me erupts into flames. The fire in the doorway has spread its way up to the ceiling.

"You're going to jail for this!" Amy spits out nastily. She turns and runs for the stairs. I run after her, putting my hand on the banister for balance. Exactly as I feared, I can feel myself starting to lose control. With this dangerous medley of emotions stirring inside of me, my hands shake, my heart thumps heavily in my chest.

"Wait!" I cry. The hand on the banister flares and the railing catches fire. The fire spreads faster than I can process, eating up the ragged walls. Amy reaches the front door. Overwhelmed and not thinking straight I throw my hand out desperately.

"Stop!" Fire hits the door and rises. Amy screams. I am not the bad guy. Her words drift to the forefront of my mind. Right now I can't help but feel that I am. I've already caused so much damage. And I can't stop. Amy rushes for the back door down the hall. I rush down the stairs, almost floating above the steps and I descend. I shoot fire past my mother intentionally, desperately wanting her to stop running away from me. The fire hits the floor, blocking the passage down the hallway and trapping her between me and the brand-new wall of flames. My mom turns slowly to face me.

"Please!" I choke. "I can't go to jail. I don't even know why any of this is happening. I don't know how any of this is possible."

"You know, your father always said you had potential to be something great. But look at you now, you're nothing but a monster." My mother's voice has become raspy from the smoke in the air. I can feel tension in my chest but I know it's not the smoke affecting me. "And now we're both gonna die. Are you happy? Is this what you wanted? Well, your father was wrong in everything he said about you. And if I die now then at least I won't have to live with the slut that you are."

The last few words reverberate in my mind. The ticking time-bomb that is my heart — wired with hurt, with stress, with anxiety, with confusion, with a great sense of injustice finally detonates. I scream at the top of my lungs and the entire room explodes into fire. There is a despairingly loud creaking above. The whole top floor has been consumed, weakened and torn apart by the element. Then ceiling collapses on top of Mom.

I am paralyzed for a moment by what just happened. Then my eyes widen when I see her lying under a pile of rubble, unmoving. I run over to her and check her pulse. My stomach clenches as my heart falls into it. She is dead. I breath heavily with the realization that I have killed my mother. I back away slowly, horrified at what I've done. In truth, I wish I could back away out of my own body, leave this turbulent vessel behind. I am horrified at myself. I run out of the front door, grasping the searing handle with ease and run out of the front door. Choking sobs escape, and with tears running down my face, I grab my bike off the overgrown front lawn and start towards Caitlin's house, leaving everything behind for good.

I jump off my bike as soon as I reach Caitlin's front yard. I run to the door and am about to knock when I realize that it's nearly ten p.m. I can wake Caitlin, but I wouldn't dare wake her parents. I don't want them involved in this mess, so I pull out my phone and text Caitlin that I'm at her door. I notice that my phone is almost out of battery. Antsy, I wait for the door to open. Soon, Caitlin appears in front of me.

"Sam!" Caitlin's face is overrun with concern and bewilderment. Her eyes scan me quickly and now she looks scared too. It dawns on me for a moment that I must look awful; covered in soot, disheveled, tear stains running down my face. "Sam, what's going on —" Her sentence is cut off when I push past her into the house. The only time I have ever welcomed myself in.

"I have to talk to you."

"Okay. But quiet, my parents are asleep," she says quietly.

"That's why I texted you." I notice Caitlin's eyes flick as she tries to assimilate the situation. I quietly take the stairs two at a time up to Caitlin's room. The sound of her footsteps follow mine. We sit on her bed, facing each other cross legged as if we're having a sleepover, except Caitlin is the only one in her pjs, and it's the farthest thing from a sleepover. Caitlin listens attentively as I explain what happened, trying to keep my voice steady as Caitlin's face grows pale. When I finish, she sits quietly for a few seconds, processing everything.

"She's really dead?" I have never seen Caitlin so grieved before. I nod. Now that I'm sitting and I've spilled it all out, the weight of my position really begins to fall on me. I suddenly find it hard to breathe. Caitlin notices and places a hand on my shoulder. "Hey, Sam, take a deep breath. I know this is a lot but try to stay calm okay?" she says, more for the both of us.

I look at her in the eyes as I take a few breaths in and out, which she does with me. I appreciate Caitlin trying to reign me back in even though she is just as shocked as I am. A thought hits me and I bounce off Caitlin's bed abruptly. Caitlin watches as I leave her bedroom and head downstairs. In the living room I grab a remote and turn on the TV, making sure the volume stays low. I flip through a few channels until I land on one showing my house, crumbling and dripping wet as firefighters hose it down. A reporter interviews an old lady. I never did learn my neighbours' names, we've always just gone about our own things. Besides, she would just be another person to try to hide my home life from... Can't have that. In the background, two firefighters roll a stretcher towards an ambulance with what I know is my mother's body under a blanket. I shudder. My neighbour speaks into the mic held in front of her.

"I went to take the trash out and, good heavens, the whole house was up in flames! I called the firehouse as soon as I could get my hands on a phone."

"Do you know if Mrs..." the interviewer's voice trails.

"Grace, I believe," my neighbour interjects. "I've never talked to her much, she's always in and out, so busy."

"Do you know if Mrs. Grace had anyone else living with her?"

"Oh, yes. Her young daughter, she bikes to school every day." I want to curse that old lady. I know she's just answering the questions, but of all the times she's minded her own business, this is the one time it matters. The firefighters would have checked the house and found no one there but my mother and, knowing that she had a daughter who was effectively not present, they may begin to assume the worst. I quickly turn off the TV, feeling panic rise inside me again. I turn and see Caitlin standing behind the couch, her eyes move from the blank TV screen to meet mine. We're thinking the same thing.

"Sam, as soon as the police find out you've run away, they'll accuse you of murder. You have to get out of the city. Now." It occurs to me that we could say I went out for a late sleepover, but if they questioned Caitlin's parents they would soon find out we had never planned a sleepover to begin with and that would make me look suspicious. With growing sorrow, I realize Caitlin is right, and nod grimly.

Caitlin sweeps through the kitchen gathering granola bars and money from the family emergency jar and piles them into my hands. I stuff the items into my sweater pockets. At the front door, we exchange an anxious gaze. Caitlin is the first to speak.

"Be safe, okay, Sam. 'Cause I swear if something happened to you..." This is the most serious I have seen Caitlin since I've known her.

I suppress the tension building inside for Caitlin's sake. "'Cait, don't think that way, it'll just make it worse..." I say and my jaw tightens. I wish I could say something reassuring, ease her anxiety, but I got nothing in me. Instead, I step in for a hug before turning to leave.

"Keep in touch, okay!" she calls after me quietly, wringing her hands.

"I will." But even as I say it, I know it will be harder to do so than I think. My phone won't survive much longer with only twenty-five percent battery left. I pull my bike off the lawn and look back one last time. I climb onto my bicycle and try to hold on to the tiny bit of hope I've just felt when I looked at Caitlin's face. That's a little bit I have to stretch out and make last for who knows how long. I thrust my foot down on the pedal and bike the fastest I ever have.

Chapter 5

Leaning my beloved bike against the side of the subway entrance, I try to pretend I don't feel sad knowing that I probably won't ever see it again. This vehicle was the symbol of freedom for me. It took me anywhere I wanted to go, it was my easy escape whenever I needed to get out of the house... Now I don't have a house, and I have no choice but to leave my bike behind. I trot down into the underground. Thankfully, the landing isn't very crowded this late. I wait about fifteen minutes. I've only ever taken the subway a few times, and that was when I was younger, with my dad. When I was seven, I believe, we had taken a weekend trip to Calgary and visited its Military Museum. Unlike me, my dad had been enthralled, but I had gone because I had wanted to spend time with him. Now Calgary is exactly where I am headed. It's the only other place I am even remotely familiar with. It's within the same province but far enough away from the mess I've made in Edmonton.

When the train arrives, I board, glancing around nervously. I wonder how many of these people have watched the news. Likely not many of them. I force myself to act normal, doing otherwise would make me look suspicious for nothing. I sit in a seat at the back, hoping to distance myself from the other passengers. I lean my head against the window as I wait for the transport to start its four-hour journey. I lift my hand to my chest and fiddle with the flower pendant. I was eight years old when my dad gave me this necklace, less than a year before he left. The gift should have felt like a betrayal, a weak apology for abandoning our family, but he was better than Mom, and in a way I can't blame him for leaving her, even if that meant leaving me behind too. That doesn't mean I'm not mad at him, though. He still left me in an awful situation that would only continue to spiral downward. I guess the necklace is just a reminder of the good memories I have with him, when things were more-or-less alright.

"I have something for you," he said. He crouched down to my level and opened a small box. The flower lay on a black felt cushion. I was delighted. He closed the clasp around the back of my neck for me. He smoothed my hair back into place and looked at me in the eyes and said, "no matter where I am, I will always be with you." I smiled and hugged him. A nice moment, but it's a little bitter now. I wonder if he ever thinks back on what he had said to me that day. Does he ever regret leaving? And lying to me? My thoughts begin to numb and my heavy eyes slowly close.

Four and a half hours later the subway train screeches to a halt. The sound of shuffling ahead of me arouses me from sleep. I stand and stretch out my stiffness, then examine my phone screen. It's around three in the morning, and my battery is now down to eleven percent. Great. I step out into the chilly air at the Calgary subway station. Shadows wash over the concrete walls. A wrapper and a flyer blow across the floor. I stroll up the stairs into the open night air, stars barely visible. That's what I've always found unfortunate about light pollution.

I find a bench near the subway entrance and sit on the cool metal. I put my hands in my sweater pockets and watch as few people walk by. Some late-nighters, but mostly those who got off the train with me. I hear a scuffling sound to my right and turn to look. An old man walks over and sits on the other end of the bench. He smiles at me drunkenly and seems to want to slide over closer to me. Instinctively I put a hand down between us. I watch as the man's smile fades and a muddled look begins to form on his face. Suddenly he jumps off the bench clutching his butt and turns to look at me with a horrified and confused expression. He staggers away. Perplexed, I look down, and sigh when I realize what happened. A red glow has spread onto the bench from my hand to where the man was sitting a second ago. I pull my hand away and hold it in the other one. I can't do things like this here. Not in public. Not with the police looking for me. I lean back and know this is going to be the longest and possibly coldest night of my life.

I wake up a little disoriented. My heart drops when I realize I've dozed off again. All this stress has knocked the energy right out of me. I don't remember much after five thirty this morning so that's when I must have passed out. I look at my phone, the battery has dropped faster due to the cold, now at four percent. It's also seven in the morning and I'm suddenly very aware of the eyes around me. Early risers out for walks and people off to the subway station for work throw glances as they pass by. They must think I passed out drunk on the park bench overnight. A rebellious teenager. Maybe even delinquent. Then all the detail of my circumstance rushes back and it suddenly occurs to me that any of these people may have watched the news. What exactly does it say about me now? I have to find out, and quickly.

I thrust myself off the park bench and march down the street in search of a shop with an open sign. I find a Starbucks two streets down from the Subway. There is already a small lineup at the counter. I wait in line and ask for a glass of water when it's my turn. I drink it gratefully on my way to a corner table. I look up at the wall mounted TV, which is set to a news channel. I watch the screen carefully for any updates back in Edmonton. I almost choke on my water when a picture of me pops open with the caption: Suspect in Murder of Mother.

"Shit," I mutter.

After inspecting the house, they must have found that the fire originated in my bedroom. They will have also discovered by now the hand-shaped marks burnt into my mother's arms — of course I'm a suspect. It still takes me off guard. I never thought I would ever find myself in this kind of trouble. I skim over the room and notice that some customers are beginning to make a connection between me and the murder suspect. I chug the rest of my water and leave the cafe immediately.

I make my way down the street and, just my luck, it begins to rain. I glance up at the grey sky and, deciding to wait it out, slip under the arched entrance of a public parking facility. I can't help my eyes shooting every which way in paranoia. Large drops fall from the sky making the morning gloomy and downcast. I lean against a wall and pull my hood over my head. My fingers instinctively find themselves on my necklace for comfort, which makes me think of my dad. He is now my only family, and all I know about him is that he moved to New York. He left, but I have a feeling he once really cared about me based on the memories I have of him from my childhood. Maybe I can find him, ask for help. I don't know how he would react when I tell him what happened in Edmonton, that his ex-wife is now dead, because of me, too. I don't even know if he would be happy to see me in the first place. Maybe he has completely moved on and left the thought of his old family in the past. If I went to him, I would be counting everything on the possibility that he might actually want to see me again, and that he might want to help me. Even then, would he be able to help? How? So many questions. So many uncertainties.

I skim my surroundings before pulling out my phone. It's a risk, but I have nothing to lose. I open Google and type in my father's name: James Craig. I follow up my search entry with the only other thing I know about him — his career as scientist. He must have become successful enough since I easily find a profile on him. I click the link and find that his work is based in biology, and that he works in a laboratory complex in Washington DC. If I can somehow get into the complex, I might be able to ask for him and then we could talk. I read the blocks of text underneath my father's picture and title. They provide information on some of his innovative projects and renown contributions to DUSSAL Labs, his workplace. I read that he has quickly risen in the organization, overseeing and regulating his own projects within his department. If he understands my situation, maybe he'll agree to help me, prove that I'm innocent. Again, I find myself asking how. Especially if I refuse to reveal the truth of my situation, about my supernatural ability.

I decide that this question can be dealt with later. One step at a time. First, I have to find a ride to Washington. I open a new page on Google and am about to search the subway schedule when my screen suddenly goes dark. My battery has finally run out. I sigh in frustration. That means I now have to go back to the subway station and look at the physical schedule. I would have had to go back anyway to purchase a ticket at the booth since I only have money in cash. The rain finally stops. I pocket my phone and leave my shelter, and that's when I realize with a startle that I should contact Caitlin to let her know that I've made it to Calgary and that I'm okay. For that I have to use someone else's phone. I make my way down the street when I see a police car pull up on the other side somewhere behind me. I watch closely as a police officer exits the vehicle. I try to fight a sense of paranoia. The officer crosses the street. I whisper to myself to stay calm and keep walking casually. She enters the Starbucks I had left earlier. I let out a sigh of relief.

Reluctantly, I risk walking into a Vietnamese fast-food restaurant. The air smells like broth and vegetables. Even though it's morning, the space feels dark, most likely due to the interior of the restaurant being designed largely in the colour black. I cautiously make my way to the counter.

"Do you think I could use your phone?" I ask the cashier. The employee, a young Asian girl, inattentively hands me the restaurant phone then turns around and begins to talk to her female coworker.

I make my way to a secluded corner of the restaurant and dial Caitlin's number. She is practically the only contact in my phone so inevitably — and thankfully — I have memorized her number. I put the phone to my ear and glance around nervously. The phone rings for what feel like forever.

"Come on, Caitlin, pick up. Pick up."

"Hello?" I hear Caitlin's voice on the other end of the line.

"Cait, it's me."

"Sam? Are you okay?"

"I'm okay, but it's getting harder to go unseen, people are starting to notice."

"Listen, I saw on the news that the police have been searching Edmonton all morning, soon they'll find out that you've left the city. You need to stay out of sight as much as possible."

"I will. And I think I have a plan."

"You do? What plan — What's your plan?"

"I'm going to find my dad. I looked it up, he lives in Washington DC, or at least, he works there. I'll figure out the train schedule and see if I can take a direct trip to

DC, probably take a taxi from there." There is silence on Caitlin's end for a moment.

"Okay. Wow," Caitlin says finally. "You're finally gonna see your dad again. Well, I'm glad you're okay. And look, I know it's going to get harder to stay in touch, but I'll be keeping an eye on the news for you, okay?"

"Thanks Cait. I miss you."

"I miss you too."

"I should probably go now."

"Okay, stay safe."

"I'll certainly try my best." I hang up and sigh. I return the phone and head back into the street. Just as I exit the restaurant I realize it would have been a good idea to ask Caitlin to look up the train schedule for me in advance, but it's too late now. I'm not going back in there. Since I have nothing else to do besides stick to the shadows, to the train station it is.

I descend into the train station cautiously. I see a board with a posting of the train schedule in the distance, and a map above it depicting the different trails. I approach and examine it. My heart drops when I don't find what I'm looking for. There is no direct route from Calgary to DC. The closest stop to my desired destination is Montreal, which departs tomorrow evening. I glance back at the ticket booth hoping I can find help there. The lady at the counter looks bored. I advance.

"Um, excuse me." The lady looks up at me sluggishly. "Is there a train from Montreal to DC do you think?" The lady holds eye contact with me for a moment. Her skin and brown hair are pale. She wears a thick pink sweater, a gold necklace sitting on her chest. A double chin hangs down below her face. Her cheeks are shiny like the frames of her glasses. I avert my eyes and then look at her again quickly, nervous.

"There usually is, yes," the lady answers. A two-part trip. That shouldn't slow me down too much.

"Okay. One ticket to Montreal, please."

"That will be a hundred and sixty-four dollars."

My mouth falls open slightly. I have never had to pay for a trip before, and I think it's mostly that I didn't know what kind of price to expect that caused my astonishment. I get over it quickly and reach into my hoodie, pulling out a wad of cash. While the lady counts the money I've given her, I briskly count the rest of my bundle. I have about two hundred dollars left... Geez, how much did you give me?! Well, that should be enough to afford a train from Montreal to DC and then to take me to DUSSAL by taxi. I put away the money and look up to see my ticket to Montreal slide over the counter before me.

"Enjoy your trip," says the booth-lady.

"Thanks." I take the ticket and leave.

It's night now. I sit in an alleyway with my back leaning against a brick wall, all my insecurity screaming at me. The only speck of hope I hold on to is that I now have a plan. The ticket is purchased, all I have to do is get on the train tomorrow evening. I'll figure out the next trip scheduled to leave for DC once I get to Montreal. One step at a time. That's the only way I can move forward without overwhelming myself. I pull one of the granola bars Caitlin gave me out of my hoodie and swallow two anxiety pills with my snack, then place the empty rapper on the ground beside me. I am suddenly aware that I am shivering. I cast a wary glance to either side of the alley way, then open my hand to produce a flame. It may be a pitiful attempt to warm myself, but it's an attempt regardless. Once the fire grows in my palm, I feel warmth fall over my entire body, as if using my power causes my body to adapt to the weather. Maybe it does. There are still so many things I don't know about myself now. It's like I don't understand myself anymore. My body has morphed into something new and impossible. I feel like a baby who learns every day that it has hands, and a voice, and is surprised at its discoveries. What else can it do? What else does it possess? I stare at the miracle in my hand. The scene with my mom comes flashing back into my mind.

Look at you now, you're nothing but a monster. The ceiling crashes down on my mom. I can still feel the horror I felt when I realize my mother is dead, and that it's my fault. Suddenly it feels like the warmth has left me. I close my hand, extinguishing the flame. Maybe she was right. Maybe I am a monster.

Chapter 6

It is still dark out. My head jerks when I hear whispers in the distance, voices echo off the brick walls and seem to bounce around me. Nervously, I stand.

"Hello?" I call.

A small light appears far away. I squint, trying to make it out. More glowing dots begin to appear all the way down the alleyway, on either side of me. Startled, I realize they are eyes, glowing and watching me from all directions. I shriek when I feel something grab my arm. I look down to see a handcuff clamped around my wrist, my eyes following the chain up to the shadow of a police officer, his badge faintly glinting in the glow of his eyes.

"Please. I promise, I'm not a criminal." But even as the words come out I doubt everything. Technically I am. Technically I deserve this. Technically I can't explain any of what has happened without revealing the impossibility of my condition. A hand grabs my ankle. I try to yank it away but the grip is too tight. My gaze is drawn up the arm to the body it is connected to, landing on the face on my mother, patched in blots of red and black, the shadows on her face deep.

"Look what you've done," she croaks accusingly.

"I didn't mean to!" my voice cracks. Warm tears swell into my vision. My body begins to glow red. Fire climbs up the walls on either side of me. I struggle against the gripping hands, but more emerge from the darkness and reach out for me. Fire begins to explode out of me uncontrollably. My eyes turn to fire and engulf my face. I scream.

My body jolts violently and I squeal, my chest rising and falling rapidly with each frightened breath. The sky is bright, the air is warmer. I am now aware of the stiffness in my back and legs. Pulling myself to my feet, I rub my eyes, as if trying to rub away the horrible images. Thankfully, that will be my last night in the streets.

I leave the nightmare alleyway and begin to walk down the street towards a hopefully unpopulated cafe where I can freshen up. I am about to turn into the entrance of coffee shop when I see police officers exit their vehicle with papers in hand. I immediately turn one eighty degrees and start walking the other way. I risk a glance behind me. The police officers have stopped some passers-by and ask them questions, holding up what I presume is most probably a picture of me. I slip back into my alley and cross to the other side. At the other opening I lean against the brick, thinking about what to do next. Gosh. My train is this evening. It would be tragic to not make it through the day. And even worse, if I am caught right as I'm entering the subway. No. I force myself to stop the negativity. I'll make it. I just have to try harder to lay low. I pull my hood over my head and turn onto the street. A young man passes by me just as I am leaving the alley, his shoulder bumping into mine. He spins around.

"Hey, watch where you're going."

Naturally, I turn to apologize.

"Sorry," I say quickly. Then I feel the colour drain from my face when I see his expression change.

"Hey..."

I know he has recognized me. My success at staying low lasted all of two seconds. Great job, Sam. I remind myself never to become a secret agent. I know it's only a matter of time before the guy calls the police on me, which I remember are not that far away. I turn and walk with more urgency, my body screaming for me to run, but that would only attract unnecessary attention.

I walk for what feels like forever. In reality, forever isn't far from the truth. I must have been walking for at least an hour. My calves burn with the speed at which I'm moving. Ahead of me, I see a large patch of green near a river, hemmed with trees and rocks. A sign announces it as the city's park.

I make my way across, hoping to blend in with the other park-users. I lean against a rock and inhale from my pump. A sudden worry manifests in my mind. How much oxygen do I have left in my pump? I can't get a refill. I think about how many times I use my pump daily, then try to remember when I got my latest refill. What — a couple of weeks ago? That means there mustn't be much air left inside. So now I have to make this last too. Yet again, I find myself having to push negative thoughts away. I don't need the extra stress. That's when I hear dogs barking in the distance and I already feel like they're meant for me. Voices follow. I look at my surroundings and spot a group of police officers with German shepherds on leashes. Inevitably my heart rate rises. One of the officers points a finger in my direction.

"There!"

I run. The barking seems to be catching up to me. They've let the dogs off their leashes, and I know for a fact I can't outrun them. I weave past a cyclist and roller-skater and look over my shoulder. A dog-walker staggers, its furry companion tugging at its leash as the German shepherds bolt past. I steer towards a cluster of trees on the river's edge, tripping on a root on my way down into the shade. The police dogs quickly close the distance between us. Almost there.

When the dogs are close enough, I cast a wall of fire before me causing them to bark and squeal. I use this opportunity to stand, the German shepherds already attempting to edge their way around the flames. I shoot more fire and then duck into some shrubs, peeking through

63

the branches. Some of the dogs have gotten burnt, with red glistening patches on their bodies. Defeated, they finally flee. I feel bad for the poor things, they were just doing their job, but I had no choice but to defend myself. It was either that or I would be pinned down by teeth and claws and then dragged to the police station. Through the shrubs I catch the police officers glancing at each other as their furry partners run back to them with their tails between their legs. One gestures to the rest to move into the trees. I look about me in alarm. Where can I hide where they won't find me? An idea sparks into my mind.

A few moments later, I watch the officers and their companions move into the area where I had just been. I perceive their shock at the sight of fire. One unclips his radio.

"We've got a 904 in Stanley Park, west side, near the river. Request for backup." The police officers continue forward without ever looking up. Thank God. I can feel myself slipping, my fingers aching as their grip the bark. I wait until I can no longer see them, then, exhaling in relief, I lower myself from the tree that saved my life.

I thought time tended to drag on at school sometimes, but this has definitely been the longest day of my life. I am grateful for the setting sun which will provide a bit more cover from the straining public eye. I make my way down the subway platform to find a place to wait for the train. My next finger-crossing thought is that the police haven't shut down transportation. I can't be that important. I'm just a suspect right? A suspect... in a murder case. I sigh. I glance over at the ticket booth and see that it's a different employee than yesterday. Maybe the police department haven't thought of searching the subway's ticket sale history yet. I start to feel anxious. I am so close. All I have to do is get on the train and then I can finally leave this ordeal.

I find a spot near an exit with dim lighting and loiter

impatiently. Faint echoes bounce around the underground. A few shuffling feet. A sniff. A light breeze carrying a wrapper across the concrete platform. A growing sense of unease spreads over me. I decide it's just the quietness of the subway, and the great shadows created by the mounted lights. Without warning, I am grabbed from behind. I flail immediately, fighting against my captor. Captors. A scream rises in my throat, but a man appears at my left and covers my mouth with a soaked cloth. I breathe in a sweet scent and then my vision goes black.

Chapter 7

I wake up with a drowsy head, and notice my sight is blocked by something dark. A sheet? No, there must be a bag on my head. I blink repeatedly, trying to clear some of the blurriness in my vision. I try to lift my hands, but I can't separate them. I look down through the opening around my neck and see that my hands are tied together and covered in a thick cloth, secured at the wrists. I try to use my power, but I feel the fire die almost as soon as it starts. Fireproof. I rotate my head and just barely catch a glimpse of my seat, grey and cushioned. Buttons line the inside of the arms. I listen. I hear a humming all around me, like the muffled sound of a strong engine. Am I on a plane? Then I hear a man's voice somewhere nearby.

"Where are you taking me?" I dare. I wait for a response, straining to see through the bag. No one answers me. I sag into my seat a little and wait.

I am led out of the plane and into a building. I try to focus on gathering information with my ears. Metal doors closing, echoing footsteps — we must be in a hallway. Another door. A hand pushes down on my shoulder and now I am sitting in a chair. Finally, the bag is taken off my head. I squint as my eyes welcome light again. Once my eyes adjust, they hardly believe what they see.

"Dad?"

He watches me from across a large wooden desk with files neatly organized on its surface. My kidnappers remove the cloth and ropes from my hands. I rub my wrists and examine my father's face. Last time I saw him I was eight. He was thirty-five then, and I can see that some of his wrinkles have deepened. A subtle grey streaks the sides of his hair. I thought I would feel somewhat glad to see him again when I envisioned myself getting here on my own and hopefully being allowed to knock on his office door. But right now all I feel is shocked and confused.

"Hello Samantha."

"I don't understand," is all I can manage.

"Welcome to DUSSAL Labs, a federal research centre."

"I know this place. I was on my way to see you actually, before you kidnapped me. Thanks for the free ride, would've been more comfortable without the bag on my head though. How did you find me anyway?"

"You remember that necklace I gave you before I left?" I don't say anything. I have all these pieces of information in my head and none of them seem to fit together. "It's a tracker." I look down at my beloved red flower pendant and touch it. My dad has been tracking me all this time? Why? I don't think I have felt more confused in my entire life. James notices the look on my face and continues. "You see, I've been watching over you ever since I left." The white-washed walls seem to shift out of focus around me.

"Watching. From a safe distance while I had to put up with Mom for the last seven years."

"I regret having left you, but look at how much stronger it has made you —"

"Stronger in what way?" I am not at all fooled by his mock empathy. Who does that to their kid? Who leaves them with an abusive drug addict and then tracks them for years? "The only thing that changed when you left is that I've learned to distrust the people who I thought loved me. You're just proving me right."

"I know you must have many questions —"

"And I have the right to receive answers, especially from you. Let's start with this: why didn't you fight for me? Why didn't you come back?"

James sighs. *Sighs.* As if he knew he would have to explain everything to me but it's more like a chore than extending a basic right. "Your mother had many issues, as you well know. I offered her a new life in New York, but she and I disagreed on the direction of our future together, and she refused to get help, not for me, not for our family. I had no choice but to leave. I had already been working for DUSSAL Labs for years, working on my own biochemical research from home. I was going to return to New York when I was offered a promotion. Turns out my research caught the interest of many of DUSSAL's experienced chemists. They launched an official project and put me in charge of overseeing the creation of my drug and the human trials."

"Too busy working on a drug to think twice about me? What kind of work could be more important than your own daughter?"

James sighs again. I find myself becoming more impatient with him. Every time he opens his mouth the image I've preserved of him from my childhood fades a little more. "Your defensive tone is making it difficult to talk to you, Sam," he says patiently. "I know you're upset, with reason, but once I explain why I didn't come back for you, everything will make sense. I promise."

"Explain, then! What are you waiting for?"

"I will after we check the status of your health. It's very important. Please, Sam. Very soon, we will sit together, and I will tell you everything."

"But —"

"Cooperating will only make things easier for all of us." Before I can protest any more, the agents who have been standing by the door this whole time walk over and gesture for me to stand up. I look at them begrudgingly. I rise out of my chair and glare at James one last time.

"You owe me a hundred and sixty-four dollars, by the way. Never got to use that ticket to Montreal." I turn and let the agents lead me out of the room.

Once again I am guided through a maze of hallways, but now I can see. All the walls are white and clean, everything screams "laboratory." Fluorescent lights run down the center of the ceiling. Every door is mounted with a small silver plaque with a person's name or the name of the room. Bathroom. G. Bennett. D. Farooqi. Dr. Burton. Storage. We pass by a door with a plaque reading 'Dr. Wilson' and then we stop. I read the plaque, 'Examination Room' before the door opens in front of me. I walk in.

The room is large, clean, and white like everything else. Near the far-left corner another door leads into an attached room. That must lead to Dr. Wilson's office. A few machines line the left wall, I recognize an x-ray machine. Along the back wall runs a counter with paper towels, a sink, cups, and jars filled with cotton swabs and cotton sticks. The far-right corner is boxed in with walls and a door, slightly ajar to reveal a toilet. Against the wall on the right of the room is a black leather bench with a curtain around it, hanging from a ceiling-mounted rack. A metal table on wheels sits near the bench, adorned with an array of medical tools. A man wearing a lab coat, in his fifties I assume, enters the room through the connected door.

"Sam. Please sit," he looks up from a clipboard as if he was previously analyzing information he already has about me, which is somehow not I that surprising.

"What are we doing?" I ask.

"I'm going to take a sample for a blood test." Dr. Wilson gestures to the bench. I sit reluctantly. He puts his clipboard down on the trolley and I catch a faint glimpse of my name typed on the top of the page. The doctor lifts a needle connected to a tube curbing its way into a small vile. I roll up my sleeve and let him swab my arm. "This might sting a little." I watch, unfazed, as the needle enters my arm. Blood rises in the tube and pours quickly into the small vile — except it's not red. It's murky brown. I look up and, to my dismay, see the shocked look on Dr. Wilson's face.

"Good god," he breathes. My heart drops. The needle is pulled out and replaced with a little round bandage. My mind begins to bring forward all of the worst possibilities.

"What's wrong — why is it brown? Am I dying?" Dr. Wilson looks extremely concerned, but doesn't answer. That makes me feel more concerned. Great. I'm going to die at fifteen. Not gonna lie, my life hasn't been all that sweet. Sweating, Dr. Wilson puts the vile on a tray. He un-loops the stethoscope from around his neck, plugs it into his ears and places the metal end on my chest. I watch him closely, but his face reveals no new information. Dropping the stethoscope, he picks up the tray and carries it towards his office.

"Go to the sink and drink three cups of water. When you're done, we will wait twenty minutes, then I'll take a urine sample. The cup is there." Dr. Wilson points to a cup waiting by the sink. "When you're done, grab the vile on the counter and fill it up."

I follow him with my eyes. "Is everything okay?"

Again, Dr. Wilson doesn't answer. He takes the vile into his office and disappears behind the door. My eyes widen with annoyance. What is it with this place and no one telling me anything? Way to make me feel all the more lab-ratish. Don't explain anything to Sam, it's not worth it. She probably won't understand anyway. She doesn't need to know why we kidnapped her or why we're manufacturing a new drug, and what that has to do with her. I snatch a cup off the counter and fill it almost to the brim. I chug and repeat twice more. When my stomach feels full, I turn around and begin to explore the room. I approach the trolley to examine the tools. Tweezers, syringes, scalpels, a variety of scissors. I pick up a scalpel, analyze the sharpness of the blade, and also observe how shiny all the equipment is. How long has this place been running? What has my dad been up to? He mentioned a drug... What kind of drug is he creating? I wonder who knows about his project, and who approved it in the first place. I pull myself out of my thoughts. I shouldn't make speculations about something I hardly know anything about. More and more I find myself anxious to have that promised conversation with my dad, when he could finally explain to me why I'm here and why it's so important for my future, or — why I'm important to DUSSAL's future.

Twenty-five minutes later I step out of the little powder room with the vile, now full of warm yellow liquid. I place it carefully on the counter.

"Uh, doctor... I peed," I call out awkwardly towards Dr. Wilson's door. No answer. I sigh. I'm getting really sick of silence. I walk over to the bench and sit, wondering how much longer I'm going to have to wait. Just then, the office door opens and Dr. Wilson enters. With hardly a glance he grabs a gown from a basket and hands it to me.

"Change into this. We're taking an x-ray."
His seeming to be in a rush makes me think something is terribly wrong with me. He has probably seen what the drug Amy injected into me has done. Soon he'll be telling me how long I have to live. I take the gown obediently, knowing none of my questions will be answered anyway. I see Dr. Wilson entering his office with the yellow vile just as I close the curtain around myself. A moment later I stand nervously in my socks and gown with the rest of my clothing sitting on the leather bench behind me. The door opens again and Dr. Wilson makes his way to the

x-ray machine. He gestures for me to go stand in front of the white square hanging on the wall. I watch as he disappears behind the bulky screen. Tubes and wires snake out of the machine and up towards the ceiling. I realize I am shivering. The room is very air conditioned, but it's more than that... I am snapped out of my daze. Literally — the doctor snaps his fingers to get my attention. I have a name, you know.

"You can change now. There's more to do, but that will be all for today. Someone will come and get you in a few minutes." With his new photographs in hand, Dr. Wilson steps into his office, and I know this time he won't return. I change back into my clothes and dump the gown into a hamper like it's done something to me. Even my mom pays more attention to me than this. It's like I'm only half here. Just someone to be looked after while DUSSAL collects my information. The door to the examination room opens to reveal the 'someone' Dr. Wilson mentioned. A guard in a black uniform. A short-sleeved shirt, trousers and boots.

"I'll take you to your room."

"Oh, how thoughtful of you! Wouldn't want to get lost." The guard ignores my sass and waits for me to cross into the hallway.

We walk for a few minutes, and it dawns on me how huge this place is. Hallways connecting to more hallways, everything looks the same. I was kidding when I said I could get lost, but now I'm beginning to believe that I actually would. We stop at a door with a plaque reading 'guest room.' I almost laugh, and hope they don't have guests very often. The guard opens the door for me.

"You're free to visit the facility, but don't wander off too much. Lunch is at noon. The signs will tell you where to go." With that, he turns and is on his way.

"And what about that talk with my dad?" I call

after him, but he is already gone. I throw my hands up and turn into 'my room.'

Funnily enough, unlike all the rest of this building so far, the guest room is pretty tiny, but it has one thing in common with the rest in that it's just as unwelcoming. A bed lies against the wall to my right, dressed with simple, thin sheets. A small desk-table and chair sit against the wall across from the door with a cable and various extensions for charging different phones placed neatly in a basket. The grey and white walls display nothing but a clock hanging over the table, which stands on a cold, hard floor.

"Charming," I say out loud. I notice a door parallel to the foot of the bed and. I check it out and see that it's a small bathroom with grey tiles and white walls. A toilet and sink stand right beside each other, with an average-sized shower at the end. A shower probably wouldn't be a bad idea. I haven't washed up since I left home — and I stayed on the street for a couple of nights. Gosh, what has my life become?

I leave the bathroom, walk over to the table, and briefly rummage through the wire basket for an iPhone charger. I notice that there are quite a few, and once again I am annoyed at how frequently Apple changes their charging ports. What's the point? It just makes everyones' lives more inconvenient. I plug my phone in and breathe a sigh of relief to see the screen come to life again. While I wait, I sit on the bed, which is more uncomfortable than the mattress I had at home — and it had springs. I let out a large breath. Now that I've sat, I become aware of how hungry I am. Lunch at noon, huh? I reach into my pocket and pull out my last granola bar, staring at it for a minute. I hope Caitlin isn't too worried, and I wonder if her parents know she's been secretly staying in contact with me. So much has happened already since I last talked to her, and I haven't even had the time or the

74

opportunity to contact her again. Most of all, I pray she's not losing sleep over my situation especially that she needs at least nine hours of sleep to function properly...

I remember one of the few times my mom ever let me spend the weekend away from home. It was two years ago, when Caitlin and I were thirteen. I spent the night over on Friday after school and we had decided to try to stay up as late as possible. We talked, played a few board games, watched two movies, and finally fell asleep at three in the morning. The next day, Caitlin was a complete zombie. I had woken up at nine and waited for Caitlin in the living room, stomach growling, when she finally dragged herself downstairs at eleven. That afternoon we had decided to make banana nut bread. In her tiredness, Caitlin had accidentally called it 'nanana butt' bread. We lost it, rolling on the floor laughing with tears streaming down our faces and clutching our stomachs for ten minutes. Mrs. Moore had passed by the kitchen and given us a confused look which only added to the humour.

The memory makes me chuckle out loud. I miss her. Why did my life have to change so drastically all of a sudden? I take a bite out of my granola bar. I promise myself that I will call Caitlin as soon as my phone is charged enough.

Putting the wrapper aside, I get up and leave the room. Time for a bit of exploring.

Chapter 8

Exploring was a bit of an exaggeration, seeing as everything pretty much looks the same. I move through one monotonous hallway after another until — How refreshing, a large open area with elevated ceilings. Floor-to-ceiling windows on one side lets in more light than the rest of the building combined, washing over modern-looking lounge areas of couches and tables. At the other end, a sort of cafeteria with black wooden tables and metal chairs. By far the coziest place at DUSSAL Labs, this room still radiates a cold unwelcome. I now notice a single guard standing still at the opposite end of the room, looking dully into the distance. Then I examine the walls and see several cameras installed at various points around the room, catching every angle. On the wall across from the windows hangs a gigantic clock which shows that it's just about eleven thirty. I ignore the growling in my stomach, move across the room, and casually walk past the guard, eyeing him cautiously in my peripheral vision. He glances at me but doesn't budge. Moving on, I find another guest room like mine and stop in front it, putting my ear to the door. It sounds empty. I wonder how many times these guest rooms have been used, and doubt that they have ever all been occupied at once. I keep going a little further and notice a set of grey double doors with a plaque that reads: CHEMISTRY LABORATORY. I try to peak through the crack between the doors but I see nothing. I am about to continue on when I suddenly decide I don't feel like getting lost and turn back towards the lounge.

Back in the sun-lit room I take a seat on one of the leather couches which is surprisingly more comfortable than it looks, and lace my fingers together, leaning back. I don't think I have done this much waiting in my entire life. I've gotten short breaks and then it's just more waiting; waiting through the night in the streets, waiting for the next subway, waiting for answers. I glance at the clock. It's twenty to noon. Now I'm waiting for lunch.

A shutter lifts, revealing an opening between the lounge and the kitchen. Sandwiches, soups, and more of the like are placed on the serving counter along with jugs of steaming coffee. Finally! I load up a tray, throwing in some utensils and napkins, and carry the whole to a table. I only remember being this hungry one other time. Last year, during an excruciatingly long presentation in the school auditorium, I could feel my stomach progressively shrink, and I shrinking into my seat along with it. When I'd finally gotten home, I had wolfed down snack after snack with tears running down my face, my stomach painfully expanding with every bite. Since then, I have always packed extra snacks.

Before I know it, my food is almost all gone. I perceive movement out of the corner of my eye and look around to see a guard approaching me.

"Finish your lunch. Mr. Craig has asked you to meet him at the gymnasium," he announces.

"What, a father- daughter work out session?"

The guard ignores the comment and steps away to wait for me at the hallway entrance. I gobble down my last few bites of sandwich and then bring my tray back to the counter. As I near the guard, he turns and leads the way.

We pass the section where I had turned around earlier. Turn right here, turn left there, and just as I begin to lose track of where we came from, we stop. The guard opens large grey doors like the ones to the chemistry lab and I enter. I am once again amazed at the size of the rooms in this building. The floor is covered in a sort of hard rubber, the walls covered in sheets of metal lined with several holes and nozzles. I notice the ceiling has similar apertures along with sprinklers and lights. Over to one side, a glass window displays the inside of some kind of observation room, its door directly beside it. I squint and see some people in lab coats sitting in front of monitors, already typing away. I suddenly notice that the room has been set with several materials like wood and metal in different sizes and types. James steps forward to greet me.

"Good lunch?"

"A little bitter," I say.

"Sam, this division is dedicated to helping us test and monitor the use of supernatural abilities, like yours."

I try to guess if he expects me to be impressed, but really all it does is make me skeptical. He seems to know a heck of a lot about what has happened to me in the past few days which makes me think he has been doing more than just 'tracking' me. Developing a drug. A room made for testing powers. My future at DUSSAL. The information is starting to come together, but I still can't figure out why or how he would have a part in what happened to me.

"Do you have something to do with my powers? Is that what you meant when you said you were developing a new drug?"

"I know you're anxious for our talk, but if you would allow me, I would like to see your power in action."

"You don't get to see anything until I know why I'm being put through all these tests in the first place."

"I promised you we would talk, and I don't break my promises. But before we can talk, we need to complete these last trials." The word 'trial' triggers the anger in me again. I really am just an un-consenting lab-rat. I've already decided that whatever he wants from me I won't be accepting.

"That's not fair! I deserve to know what's happening before I do anything for you."

"Don't test my patience, Sam. I understand how you must be feeling. I am asking you now, I would hate to have to force you."

I try to push down the anger swelling up inside me. Test his patience? He has no idea how I'm feeling. And everything has been forced on me since I got here, including getting here. If I want answers I have to go along. I have no choice anyway. He's not asking, he's telling me.

"Fine. Fine! What do you want me to do?"

"Good. We want to test your limits. These materials around you are for this purpose. For example, how quickly can you burn wood? What is your absolute? How long would it take you to melt through metal? Let's get started."

This training session is nothing like the one I had with Caitlin, whose knowledge was based on comic books — this is very scientific. I am asked to set fire to many different things: plastics, metals, wood, fabrics. I concentrate on a large sheet of metal and send a wave of fire its way. A red glow begins to form in the middle and spreads. The metal thins and finally melts, leaving a dripping gap. The entire time, I am being instructed from the observation room. "Flame," "shoot," "blaze," "fire stream," each word corresponding to a specific action which I am to do.

'Flame' is like the way fire starts when you flick a lighter or scratch a matchstick — a gentle, light flame. 'Shoot' obviously means I am to shoot a ball of fire. 'Blaze' is like 'flame' but with a more intense and enthusiastic flame, like a campfire or a furnace. 'Fire stream' is when I am to hold a steady stream of fire kind of like a flame thrower.

The difficulty of producing each of these actions go in that order, fire stream being the most exhausting. It takes so much energy, focus, and whatever else my body does to actually produce fire. The small, chubby man speaks into his microphone again, his voice projecting from a wall-mounted speaker above the observation window.

"Flame."

I place my hand on a large block of wood. Fire creeps its way down from my hand. I step back, and soon the flames consume the whole surface of the wood.

"Extinguisher," I hear the man say away from the mic. Another scientist presses a button and a spray of foam hits me from the right. The word had been spoken before, but the spray had always landed on the objects I had set fire to, in preparation for the next exercise — unless the test was to see how long I could hold a stream of fire, and how long, in relation, it would take for said object to melt or disintegrate. I look down and see that I had set fire to my sleeve without noticing. Now the arm of my sweater shows a crispy hole covered in foam. I look at the wall and see the nozzle from which the foam spray shot out. This room has been fully equipped and prepared for anything, it seems. If the drug I received did somehow make its way to me from my dad, he had chosen fire for me from the start. He had planned everything, every detail.

"Sam," says my dad's voice. "Stay focused, we still have lots of work to do."

I take a deep breath. How much more work? The woman sitting beside the microphone man continues to type away on her keyboard, recording the results. My dad stands behind them and attentively watches, glancing at the monitors every so often.

What feels like hours later, I see my dad signal to the desk people, and suddenly there is a motorized sound all around me. A second, thicker layer of wall —covered in grills and vents — slides down from the ceiling, closing over the original walls, the corners clicking together. Even though the room is large, I start to feel claustrophobic. The room is completely sealed now which gives me the sense of being trapped. I must look worried because James speaks into the mic again.

"It's alright, Sam. We are about to conduct the last set of tests — climate adaptation. The room needs to be completely sealed for us to change the temperatures. Ready?" And without waiting for me to respond, it begins.

The grills hum to life and the room increasingly glows with a red light. I am aware that the temperature is rising, but I can't physically feel the change in my body. The red lighting is almost blinding now. I squint towards the observation window and decide I am probably hallucinating. All the eyes behind the glass have widened and are darting between monitors. Is something wrong? Beads of sweat begin to surface on my skin, and I move my hair away from my neck. I have not yet been given any instructions, so I strain my ear, and faintly hear the chubby man say something about 315 Kelvin.

"Blaze," the man says into the mic. I create a fire in my hand and now I can feel my body temperature rise. The flames turn blue and purple and I can feel a sort of tingle in my fingers. I giggle at the sight. That's new — and beautiful. That's also the hottest fire I've ever produced. I examine the window again to see very nervous and sweaty-looking scientists. The instructor looks almost afraid.

"2253 Kelvin. Her temperature is up to 316," he says out loud.

I am not familiar with this measurement but from their expressions I am guessing 316 Kelvin is very high. They look frightened by this discovery, but honestly if I'm not dead right now and I feel fine, than I'm not scared. "Reset room temp," the Mic Guy adds. His colleagues' hands move over the controls and suddenly the red glow dies away. I extinguish my blaze as the room temperature quickly decreases and finds its normal state again. A few minutes pass by where I stand awkwardly in the middle of the room, feeling my body temperature resetting as well and re-adapting to my surroundings. Next, the room begins to swell with a new blue light. My breath quickly becomes a puff of fog, and I go from comfortable to shivering in a span of a few minutes. I notice frost climbing up the metal walls, ice forms on the floor around me. I take a few steps back, trying to keep my feet from freezing to the floor. My skin turns pale, my fingers shrink. The tip of my nose begins to sting with cold.

"233 Kelvin? Have her blaze." I faintly hear my dad say cooly from behind the scientists.

"Blaze," the Mic Guy's voice projects clearly.

I raise my hand again and create a blaze. The woman clicks away at her keyboard with the other watching the controls. They whisper to each other. I start to feel warmer, then I see the steam curling off of me on all sides, my internal temperature countering the external one. The scientists look at each other and nod in some kind of agreement. The blue light shuts off and the room temperature rises rapidly back to average. I put my fire out again, my hands still shaking, but I know it's not because of the cold anymore. I'm exhausted.

"Good," the Mic Guy says. The second set of metallic walls lifts back into the ceiling. James leaves the observation room and walks towards me.

"You've done a tremendous job, Sam. More to be done, of course, but you may go rest now. We'll talk tomorrow."

I look at him in annoyance and head for the exit. My knee buckles on my way out. I readjust myself and walk more slowly. A guard sees me out and watches as I tread down the hallway to the guest room.

Chapter 9

Back in my room, I notice a set of neatly folded clothes on the bed. Someone must have left them here for me while I was in the gymnasium. I lock the door and slowly strip all of my clothes off. I pull my inhaler out of my hoodie pocket and draw a breath. What does fire use a lot of? Oxygen. The one thing I'm often low on. I look up at the wall to see that the clock reads five fifteen. Really? We were in there for five hours?! No wonder I'm beat.

I hold the clothes out in front of me. Black pants and white t-shirt. Even for me — who has no sense of style — they seem very plain, but they're not so bad, and they're clean. They even thought of throwing in a fresh pair or underwear in there. Everything is my size. For the first time I feel somewhat grateful that they know so much about me.

I go into the bathroom and turn on the shower. As I wait for the water to warm up I look into the mirror. Wow. I am covered in soot. I had never thought about that happening before. I produced so much fire today that it makes sense for this to be the side-product. I slide my fingers along my arm and smudge the blackness, creating streaks on my skin. I do the same on my face for fun. Glance over to my right, I see a stack of towels and washcloths on the vanity beside the sink. They are all white, but I know once I'm done they won't anymore. I remind myself not to feel bad since they're the ones who put me through all that in the first place. I put my hand under the water and, seeing that the temperature is to my liking, I hop in.

I don't think I've appreciated a shower more than I did just now. These past few days have brought to light all the things I had been taking for granted. I make a mental note to never take the comforts of life lightly again. Putting the fresh clothes on, I already decide I'll be keeping my hoodie, even though it's kind of gross. I read the time again, it's quarter to six meaning supper must be soon, and I'm hungry again, so I head for the lounge.

When I get there, I am hit by a wave of delicious scents. The cooks are already setting the serving counter and I grab a tray in anticipation. I wait patiently for them to finish setting the dishes down before loading my tray with roasted veggies, garlic bread, chicken, and a chunk of lasagna for good measure. Briefly, I'm astonished at the selection of foods they have, but then I remember that probably many of the employees practically live here. I wonder how many have families who only get to see them a few hours a day, or one day a week; who too frequently have to sit for meals together without their mother or father. The thought makes me sad. I sit at the same spot as I did before, but the room doesn't seem so bright anymore now that the sun has gone down, the artificial light giving the room a dim glow. I munch on, savouring every warm, saucy mouthful of pasta.

The sound of footsteps echoes through the room and I glance up to see the two women from the gymnasium walking together. They put their clipboards and files under their arms and serve themselves a portion of food. In the distance I hear them murmuring to each other, but only catch bits of their conversation: "subject fourteen," "trials," "medical examination." With their trays in hand, they cross the lounge and disappear into the hallway on the other side. Alone once again, I finish my meal as clanging dishes resonate through the empty room.

Full and sleepy, I open the door to the guest room and immediately crash. When I wake up it's around midnight... I should have forced myself to stay awake longer. I try to fall back asleep, but I know it's no use. I glance at the door, wondering if I could take a late-night walk around the hallways. I get out of bed and open the door as slowly and quietly as I can. Cautiously, I peak out into the hall. I hear footsteps just in time to close my door to a crack as a guard walks by. When I can no longer hear any trace of him or anyone else, I slip out of my room and begin my wandering. Curiously I try a few doors. They are all locked. I look up at the cameras. Are there always people watching? Is it really necessary to secure the facility like that? There barely seems to be any outside visits, and especially not at night. Nervously I look both ways and listen for any other guards. Security has to be at its lowest at this time of night, I should be fine.

I entertain myself by switching the initials on the door plaques, but none of them are that much fun, except for Boctor Durton, which sounds like something the Swedish Chef would say. I switch the letters of my own room: ruest goom. Woctor Dilson. That's what I'm calling him in my head from now on. Speaking of Wr. Dilson, I arrive at his office door. Before I even have the chance to try the lock, the door flings open without warning. I swallow my breath as I flatten myself against the hallway wall. Dr. Wilson hurries out of his office, heading the other direction without spotting me, a folder with my name on it in his hands. I wait for him to get as far as possible, then stick my foot in the doorway just as it's about to click closed, then squeeze myself through the crack.

The doctor had left his lamp on before leaving, filling the room in a soft, dim light. A large wooden desk sits at the back of the room in front of a window, everything clean and tidy. A loaded wooden bookshelf stands against the wall somewhere behind the desk. The man loves his wood. Honestly, I appreciate the contrast it creates with all the metallic modernness in the rest of the building. A few beige metal cabinets line the walls. One in particular catches my eye. I don't know why, but I feel the need to open it. I quietly pull the top drawer out and rifle through the files. Several file folders categorize not particularly interesting information. I push the drawer closed and open the one under it. This one has at least a dozen thick files inside, organized in alphabetical order. I shuffle through them. Each is labeled with a name on the top. Boyd, Lucas; Campbell, Amelia; Clinton, Trevor; Harrison, Zoe. Each name has a number beside it. I pull out the first file, Boyd's. The front of the folder is stamped with the big red word "deceased." I furrow my brows and lift the next one out. The same word appears on the front of the file. I quickly discover that all of them are marked with this doomed word except for one: Clinton's, number thirteen. I place his folder on top of the drawer and flip it open. The first page has a photograph of a middle-aged man clipped to the top, and displays his basic information:

Name: Trevor Peter Clinton
Age: 40
Sex: Male
Height: 6' 0"
Weight: 165 lbs
Health: good

I skim over the information and turn over the page. A stack of x-rays lies beneath. I look at them briefly and then turn to the next pages, finding journal entries, each one dated, and describing the subject's progress. They are lengthy and detailed, but I only run my eyes quickly over the pages. I catch words like "improvement," "healing," "degradation," and then "failure." Suddenly overwhelmed, I slap the folder closed and slip it back into the drawer. Closing the drawer carefully, I move on to the desk. The surface is practically bare. The drawers hold only a few items like pens and paper weights. Nothing very exciting. I decide I've seen enough of this office and, looking down both ends of the hallway, I step out again.

I silently hope that the cameras didn't catch me sneaking into the office, but then again, if they did, someone would have come to get me by now. Motivation sparks in me again and I turn in the direction I saw Dr. Wilson go earlier. I casually walk down the hallway, still attentive for any oncoming guards. Somewhere ahead I hear voices. I move towards the wall and wait, but they don't get any closer. They must be coming from a nearby office or something. I slowly proceed forward and stop where the voices are the loudest. I realize I am back at my father's office. I squint at the plaque: James Craig. That's it. I press my ear to the door and listen to the muffled voices.

"So what is it? What's in her blood?"

"We're not quite sure yet, a mixture of things, some of them abnormal to the human body."

"And she remains perfectly healthy?"

"So far, yes. Her DNA and tissue have been successfully mutated. We will conduct more tests tomorrow morning."

"You've done well, Clarence. When you're done with her, have her sent to my office, I would like to finally speak with her about her future here. You may leave now." The way my dad speaks to Dr. Wilson makes me realize just how 'big boss' he is, like he thinks he is above everyone. There was something a little demeaning about the way he said "you may leave now" which triggers me all over again. Footsteps approach the door on the inside. I stumble back in a hurry and begin to speed walk down the hall.

"Samantha?" Dr. Wilson's voice calls after me. I

stop in my tracks, swearing under my breath, and turn around as nonchalantly as I can. "What are you doing? It's past midnight."

"You're up too. I couldn't sleep, what's your excuse?"

Dr. Wilson looks clearly nonplussed by this retort. He opens his mouth to say something, but James speaks first.

"Bring her in, Clarence." Dr. Wilson gestures for me to enter the office. I walk past him, raising an eyebrow at him as I go in. I stand behind the guest chair in front of his desk and wait. James picks up his phone and quickly dials a number.

"Security in my office, now," he orders, then hangs up and places his phone nonchalantly on his desk. Oh no. They've seen me on the cameras. They know I was sneaking around. He's going to give me a stern talking to and then have me dragged back to the 'guest room.' He sits back in his chair and interlaces his fingers.

"Sam, how are you feeling?"

"Tired. You know, from being kidnapped, examined, tested, and all that. How are you?" I ask with utmost sarcasm.

"Sit down." I remain standing, crossing my arms. Nothing about his tone or attitude makes me want to listen to him. "Come on, Sam. You're not a child." I roll my eyes and grudgingly sit on the chair across from my dad. We stare at each other for a moment in silence. The door opens behind me and I twist around in my chair. Two guards bearing tasers enter the room and station themselves on either side of the door. I spin back around to face my dad.

"Really?"

"These men will take you back to your room when we're done our conversation," he says calmly. I, on the other hand, wonder how I could be considered so unreliable that they won't even let me see myself back to the guest room.

"Are you going to tell me what's going on now, or is there something else? Maybe a fire obstacle course?"

"I apologize for making you wait this long, but I knew your anger would enhance your performance during the tests. And, I promised we would talk, so here it is. I want you to listen to me carefully. I need you to understand the importance of my mission." I gesture for him to continue. "This drug I mentioned this morning, this is my prized creation. That is what you have in your system. That is what Amy injected you with."

"So, Mom, the drug, you were behind that? How? Why?"

"I had one of my agents approach Amy undercover and convince her to take the drug to you. It took some serious persuading, seeing as she has effectively moved onto heroine since my departure, but I'm glad to see she went through with it. See, I have always known you've had the potential to do great things. I always knew you had a place in my vision for the future, with DUSSAL. But when I left, I realized that leaving you in the care of your mother would indeed create the perfect environment needed to train you to be strong, independent, and enduring. It would make you into the ideal vessel for such a drug as I've created. I have researched, trialed, worked, and reworked this drug for over a decade. I have failed many times, but I have finally perfected it. I knew you were ultimately suited for this gift. Your conditions allowed your body to accept it more easily than anyone before. Then, when I saw the news with your old home on fire, I knew for sure it had worked on you. Now I have brought you here to offer you a place at DUSSAL. Your life will finally change for the better. And if it means anything to you, I do regret having left you at such a young age, and have thought about you every day si—"

I stand and the chair screeches behind me. The guards take a step toward me but James signals for them to stay by the door. Anger swells in my chest like a burning fire.

"I can't believe this! You've already decided my whole future and you were barely there for my past! Here I was, holding on to the few memories I had of you, thinking it was better than what I had with Mom. But you never cared about me! I'm obviously just some lab rat! And what is this all for? Why are you doing this?" Tears sting my eyes.

"I want to make the world a better place," he says simply as if that explains anything.

"With power-giving drugs? You call it a gift, but I never wanted any of this." James gives me a look as if I am being unreasonable.

"What else is there for you, Sam? Think about your life. There is no one left to take care of you. You are too young to live on your own yet. Who is even going to continue paying for your education? DUSSAL has so much more to offer than any other option. In fact, DUSSAL is your only option." My head spins and I feel sick.

"You have no right to tell me what my best option is! I don't think I need to remind you that you weren't there for the last seven years. Whatever you're offering, I'm not interested." I turn to leave but the guards block the door. Once again I turn to face James angrily.

"Where do you think you're going? This facility is highly secured. You can't leave the building without a key card. Sit down."

"No —"

"Sit!" James raises his voice. I sniff, and hesitantly sit back down. I cross my arms and wait for him to begin another pitiful speech. James interlocks his fingers again, looking far more stern now. I swallow the lump in my throat. "Give me a fair chance to lay out the offer, and then you'll understand that your purpose at DUSSAL far extends anything you could image. It's not about drugs or powers, Sam. It's about the reformation of the world. I am building an army of powerful warriors. Super-soldiers, if you will. Soldiers with abilities like no one has ever seen, like yours. You are the first one to successfully receive the drug, the first of hopefully many more. As the world continually falls apart, America will be the symbol of peace. When the Middle East continues to destroy themselves with war, when poor children continue to starve, when natural disaster continues to hit civilizations, America will be there to set things right. The world needs a saving power, a country that is developed, stable, and has the means to set order to chaos. Fire, water, medicine, strength— all these are required to clean up collapsed cities, improve nations, and create miracles for people in need. These powers will help to restore the world.

I called my work Project Wild Rose, after the drug, a flower symbolizing both beauty and pain. I want beauty to rise out of a world filled with pain. This will change the world for the better, you understand? I knew your journey would be difficult, but I also know in the end you will find joy in what your future holds. You can be a part of this. When America shows itself to be the country that everyone can depend on, the world will look to us as a saving grace."

"Sounds more like a cult than anything."

"I want you to join us," he continues as if I had made no comment. "You're incredible, Sam. You are strong-willed, you're smart, you're determined. I've always said you were capable of anything. You belong with DUSSAL. This is your chance to be something great, to be part of something that will change the world. How could anyone refuse that?

"Like this: No thanks. I don't want to see the world change at the hands of a nutcase. You don't want America to be a saving grace. It sounds more like you just want to rule the world."

He interlinks his fingers neatly over his desktop. "Take it how you will, but all I ask is that you give this more thought before you make up your mind." James looks up and addresses the guards. "Give her some time alone." I look around to see the guards move forward.

"I've already made up my mind," I tell James as I stand. "I thought I made that clear. And if free-will means anything to you, let me go."

"I can't do that."

And just like that, strong hands grip my arms and lead me out of the room. I struggle against them, attempting to wrench my arms out of their grasp. I just catch a glimpse of James, completely unfazed, going back to reading the files on his desk before I am dragged down the hall.

Chapter 10

Shoved into my room, the door is locked behind me. The fact that it's even possible to lock a guest room door from the outside in this place adds to my rage. I let out a cry of frustration and pace the room briskly. I wouldn't be surprised if I was actually fuming — I guess that's a probability now. I tear the necklace I've cherished for all of these years off my neck and throw it to the ground. One of the petals breaks off. I violently stomp on it for good measure. When I'm done, I stare down at it for a while, breathing heavily. My hands are red-hot and shaking. I close them into fists, hoping to defuse them back to normal. I sit on the bed and close my eyes. How did all this happen so quickly? My life wasn't great, but I was doing fine. I had a plan. I was going to move out after my high school graduation and, and...

I sigh and drop my face into my hands. Okay, truth is I still have no idea what I want to do with my life. To be fair, I haven't had much time to think about it lately. All I know for sure is that I'm not joining some bullshit American army attempting to take over the world. That goes against so many of my values and convictions. Who does he think he is? A hypocrite, that's who. Claiming he recognizes my value and saying I can go and 'think about it,' but he hasn't respected me in a single way, and he's already decided for me. Everything. I know he won't take no for an answer. The only question is, how do I get myself out of this? I breathe from my asthma pump and swallow two anxiety pills. I look at the bottle, there's only two pills left. I examine my pump and realize my oxygen supply is almost out, too. I curse under my breath. Just what I need right now. More problems. Okay, focus. I need a real plan. I can't just sit around and wait for them to manipulate me some more. What would Caitlin do? I think it through. Observing my surroundings, I first notice the room doesn't have a smoke detector, which will allow me to build up a collection of smoke. Next, I tear a strip from the bed sheets and wrap it around my face like a scarf. For my plan to work, I will have to rely on the smoke finding its way through the cracks of the door and being spotted by the security cameras. All I have to do now is wait.

Some time later, I hear footsteps hurry down the hallway outside the guest room door, then the shuffling stops.

"Open the door!" a male voice calls out through the door. Seconds pass by in silence, I remain still. I hear the lock turn and the door is thrown open cautiously. Smoke billows out of the room. "Come out!" the male voice speaks again. I respond with more silence. I light a small fire in my hand which shines in a blur through the smoke. I can feel their unease and it almost makes me smile. Blinking my stinging eyes, I send an explosive wave of fire out of the room and hear bodies hit the floor and wall across the hallway. A smoke detector outside my room finally rings its warning, and sprinklers go off. I step out and over an unconscious guard, pluck a key card off of a belt, and dart away to find the nearest exit.

I pull the makeshift scarf off my face as I run and chuck it to the side. As I round a corner, my asthma pump and bottle of anxiety pills bounce around in my hoodie pockets. I keep my attention on spotting any exit sign. I make another turn, already feeling like I am getting lost. There! A red glowing sign above a door indicates an exit. I totter to a stop and slide the key card across the grey metal pad on the wall. There is a click and I push the door open. Part of me wants to enjoy the fresh air but

I need to focus. The parking lot is full of cars, and the whole facility is surrounded by a tall metal wire fence. Movement in the distance catches my eye. The main gate is opening to let an employee in. A guard stands inside his booth at the gate, working the controls. The sound of shouting makes me spin around. Some guards on outdoor duty have spotted me. I glance at the arriving vehicle and run towards it. A loud bang is followed by a bullet flying past me and my heart rate accelerates. They're shooting at me?! I just reach the car as it turns into a parking spot and make my way around to the front while staying low.

"Stop shooting! I need her unharmed!" my dad's voice echoes across the pavement. I risk a glance over the side of the car. The employee, a woman in formal attire, gets out of her vehicle and I pounce. Already confused, the employee is now taken by surprise as I snatch her keys away, push her and lock myself into the driver's seat. The employee yells at me, banging on the window, and vigorously pulling at the handle, but I ignore her. Seat belt. Reverse. Gas. The car jerks backwards and my heart sinks into my stomach. The rearview mirror shows a dozen guards running in my direction or getting ready to jump into their own vehicles if necessary. I spin the wheel to the left and the car obediently turns right. The furious woman stumbles out of the way of her own car. I set the shift stick to drive and put the pedal to the metal.

"Ugh, what am I doing?" I ask myself, my heart thumping heavily in my chest. I lead the car to the gates, which are closed again. The guard steadies himself, ready to confront me. I just need enough speed and I can — The front of the car crashes into the gates and they swing open. I laugh nervously. "Highly secured my-ass."

I turn onto the main street, terrified of getting into an accident and this being all for nothing. I've never driven before. I'm only going off what I've seen in movies, and even then, it's not as easy as it looks. I quickly glance at the rearview mirror and see several black vehicles pursuing me. The next moments are the most stressful of my life. I continue to drive unsteadily down the main road, unsure where I am even going, and not knowing when I should turn. I weave in and out of traffic and pray I don't get anyone killed. The DUSSAL vehicles follow my weaving effortlessly. To my right, a bridge entrance approaches. Okay, slow down just a bit, now turn. Forgetting that flash signals are even a thing, I recklessly turn the steering wheel and barely miss a madly honking car.

On the bridge, a space clears up beside me and a black DUSSAL vehicle fills it. As if trying to match my recklessness, the driver attempts to crash into the side of my vehicle. I swerve and the passenger door scrapes along the edge of the bridge. I swerve off the concrete barrier and continue on, trying to lose my pursuer. All around me, cars honk, people yell and cuss out of their windows, veering out of the way of danger. I push down on the pedal and speed past the pursuing car. Another enemy vehicle manages to squeeze itself skillfully between my car and the edge of the bridge. Now I am sandwiched with nowhere to go but forward. I begin to hyperventilate. How did I think this was a good idea? But then, what other options did I have? Carelessly walk as far away from DUSSAL Labs as I can and see how long it takes them to catch up to me by car? Perilously, I grip the wheel with one hand and fumble in my pocket for my asthma pump with the other.

Behind me a third car closes in from the back. The guard in the driver's seat sticks his arm out of the window with a gun in his hand and shoots at my tires. I feel one of them pop and I lose control. The car jerks to the right and I crash into the side of the bridge. I stay frozen at the wheel for a moment, neck stiff, lungs tight. The DUSSAL vehicles screech to a halt around me. Guards spill out of their automobiles and close in, weapons at the ready. I force myself to snap out of it. I open the driver's door and tumble out, dazed. I run around the front of my vehicle towards the edge of the bridge when — a sharp pain in my right leg makes me cry out. I stumble but do my best to keep running. They shot me! They actually shot me!

"No! You idiot!" my father's voice yells from the distance. I look back at him one last time as I swing a leg over the concrete barricade. "Get her!" Guards approach quickly. I look at the river below, hoping and praying that the water is deep enough to catch me. I take a deep breath and with a yell, I jump.

Chapter 11

Gasping, I pull myself onto the riverbank. I cough and curl my fingers around the grass, trying to get a better grip. Weighed down by soaking clothes and exhausted I give a last bit of effort to drag myself further into the boarder of trees lining the riverside. I lean my back onto a tree. The chopping sound of a helicopter's rotator blades crosses the sky somewhere above me and fades as it continues down the river. My head drops back against the bark, grateful to be out of the water.

Bubbles violently rising above me. Freezing darkness all around. Murky water rushing into my mouth. Disoriented and running out of air, my limbs frantically flailing. Miraculously my hands breaking the surface. Cool air flooding into my lungs.

I close my eyes. The adrenalin from the car chase still runs through me, and I can feel my hands shake. I think I may have thrown getting my driver's license out the window — and I'll probably have nightmares about car chases for the rest of my life. Suddenly, pain in my leg flares up again and only now do I remember that I was shot. I look at my leg. My pants are torn across the side of my calf, exposing a red gash. It's still bleeding, my new mutated brown blood soaking the fabric around the wound. Gently, I pull my pant leg up, cringing. I take a better look... it seems like the bullet only grazed my leg. I'm relieved at first, but it occurs to me that the polluted water could have infected the wound. Calm down. One step at a time. With ever-trembling hands I pull out my pill bottle. Fortunately, my supplies didn't float out of my pockets in the river. I pour the last two pills into my wet hand and swallow them dry. Putting the empty bottle onto the grass beside me, I reach in a grab my pump. Water drips out of it. It's ruined. I pile the pill bottle and pump into my hand and throw them into the river with a grunt. I sit, panting in frustration. I want to regret my carelessness, but polluting is the least of my worries right now. Damn, everything is so messed up. I look down at my leg again. I won't get very far by limping, and I don't know how much time I have to get out of here before they find me. I have to get into the city. Actually, I have to leave it. I have a bit of money left, but only enough to take a taxi to the neighbouring city.

My science brain, as Caitlin would call it, thinks through the things I've learnt for anything useful for my leg situation. I read somewhere about cauterization being used to treat wounded soldiers. It was done usually with hot metal, and sometimes chemicals or lasers. Seeing as I don't have any other tools except for fire, I guess it's my only option. I place my fingers on the bullet graze. They begin to glow and I feel a sting coming on, then feel the wound sealing. The bleeding stops. I am immune to the heat of fire, but I guess when your flesh is torn open it's a different story. I wince, feeling the burn of my own fire for the first time. Finally, I pull my hand away. Red marks remain in the shape of my fingers around my new scar. I take a deep breath and lean back against the tree again.

I can't stay here much longer. How long have I even been sitting on the riverbank? I take out my phone to check the time. Then it hits me that it probably doesn't work. Everything seems to be playing against me right now... I try to turn it on, and to my surprise it flickers to life. I sigh in relief and look at the time. I'm going to guess it's been about fifteen minutes. I should get going. But where do I go? I don't really have a plan. I stare out at the river, shivering in my wet clothes. Who would believe my story, and then be willing to help? The only people who knew the kind of things that go on at DUSSAL and didn't work there are deceased...

Except one! Trevor Clinton! If I find him, maybe he could tell me more about DUSSAL, and then maybe I could find a way to take their whole operation down. About a dozen people died in the drug trials, just so my dad could build a super-power army and attempt to take over the world. I need to know what happened to him. If he survived and he's not working with DUSSAL anymore, then that means either he escaped or they let him go. Maybe it didn't work out the way they wanted it to? There's still so much James refuses to tell me about this drug, about... Wild Rose, and its development.

Suddenly motivated, I unlock my phone and open up the web. I type Trevor Clinton in the search bar. Surprisingly, a lot of information comes up. I press the first link, which leads me to an article on a Trevor Clinton in Washington D.C. I quickly skim over the screen, reading about Trevor's contributions to the community and to the economy as a businessman. CFO in journalism. Rose in the company very quickly. Praised for work-ethic and dedication to the company. On the side, organized and funded a public community garden. Donations to local and global charities. Oversaw a fundraiser run for special-needs students school programs. The list goes on. I go back to the main page and click another link. The headline answers part of my question. "Beloved community member and CEO, Trevor Clinton, steps down after tragic accident." Heartrate rising, I read a very vague article about an incident which left Mr. Clinton crippled. He stepped down from the company, refusing to talk about the incident at all, and then shrank back and became somewhat of a ghost to society. The article states suspicions about his having moved to Maryland. I shut my phone. That's all I need for now. Maryland seems to be the only thing I have to go on right now. Weakly, I lift myself off the ground. Limping, I head towards the city, looking like a complete mess.

I step away from the counter where a helpful and thankfully oblivious lady has just handed me a wad of American cash. When I had reached the city I realized I only had Canadian money, and if I wanted to get anywhere, I needed to swap the currency. When I had reached a public bank, I had stepped to the side and counted my remaining bills. I tried to think about what I had spent so far on travel and how much I have now, and my heart had almost momentarily stopped after realizing Caitlin had handed me almost five hundred dollars of her family's savings. I still feel bad, and I make a mental note to pay back every dime once this is all over. Now I have just about a hundred dollars left. That's enough to take a taxi to Maryland and get myself some fresh, dry clothes. I pocket my American cash and leave the bank.

I look around for a clothing store, but the States doesn't seem to have many of the brands I'm familiar with, or at least D.C. doesn't. I choose a random clothing store that I determine to be average and pick out the cheapest and simplest items I can find. I emerge wearing blue skinny jeans, a unicolored t-shirt, and a new zip-up hoodie. I dump my old wet DUSSAL clothes in a public trash can, where they belong, and wait on the side of the road, hand ready to signal a cab. A few moments later a taxi approaches and, when I wave it down, it slow to a stop in front of me and I get in. The taxi driver looks at me in the rearview mirror, waiting for directions.

"Just drop me off in Maryland," I say like an idiot.

"Where in Maryland?" the driver says, his face dull, his eyebrows raised lazily.

"I don't know, somewhere in the center," I continue and hope he understands I don't know the area.

"Baltimore?"

"Sure." I trust that Baltimore will be where I want to go. He knows what he's doing. The driver eyes me a little suspiciously. I hold up my stack of money where he can see, then he shrugs and begins to drive. I sit back and it suddenly occurs to me that I'm in a vehicle again not that long after the chase. As long as someone else is driving, I'll be fine.

About twenty minutes later the cab pulls up to the roadside, and I hand the driver the rest of my bills.

"Thank you," I say and exit the vehicle. For the first time, I notice what a beautiful morning it is. It's not too chilly, and the sun is shining brightly. For the first time in what feels like forever, my surroundings feel cheerful. People go about their own business, walking to work, making their way to shops, walking their dogs. The street is busy with cars, the sky is blue. For one second, life feels somewhat normal.

But, back to business. I pull out my phone and look up Trevor Clinton again. Now that I'm in Maryland, maybe I can find more clues as to where exactly I can find him. Maryland can't be that big, right? Out of curiosity I look up the size of Maryland and I'm surprised to find that it could fit in Alberta twenty times. I got this. Trevor could be around any street corner. I look up and realize that I'm still standing in the middle of the sidewalk with people moving out of the way to walk around me. Feeling a bit stupid, I retreat to a nearby bench. Leaning over my phone, I scroll through the web. Many T. Clintons appear but none of them feel right; Trevor Clinton Facebook profiles for a bunch of random people, but none of them are visibly disabled, so I continue my search. T. Clinton garage — nope that's a Terrance. Trevor Clinton real estate — too young. Finally, a link for 'T. Clinton, repairman' comes up. Runs a small repair shop from home, which lines up with his being disabled, if he's a small item repairman, he could very easily sit while working. The top of the page shows the address and phone number. This seems hopeful. A bit more scrolling tells me that's all the T. Clintons around this area. I decide to pursue this lead. I copy-paste the address into Google maps and see that it's a two and a half hour walk from here, and since I have no more money for a taxi, I have no choice. I sigh, remembering my sore and still-healing leg. Here we go. I get up, hold the screen in front of me and follow the blue line.

Close to three hours later, I step up to a door just off of a main street at the front of a quiet neighbourhood. A sign nailed to the wall beside the door tells me this is the right place. Exhausted and sore, I knock. Gosh, I hope this is the right person. I don't know what I would do if I came all this way to bother a stranger with still no money and nowhere to stay the night — again. I wait, my legs trembling from nervousness and fatigue. The door opens and at first all I see is empty space looking into a hallway. My eyes drift downward and land on a grey-haired, bearded man in a wheelchair. He wears a knitted cardigan-style sweater and loose jeans, with thick grey slippers on his feet.

"Who are you?" he looks up at me with a bothered air.

"I'm Sam Grace."

"Isn't Sam a guy's name?" he retorts.

"Well, it's actually Samantha, but I prefer Sam."

"What do you want?"

"Your name is Trevor right?"

"Yes. And now that we're all acquainted, you want to tell me what this is about?" he says a little impatiently.

"I was hoping we could talk about DUSSAL." His face hardens slightly when I pronounce the last word.

"There's nothing to talk about. I'm not familiar with it. Now, I have to get back to work, if you don't mind."

Trevor begins to close the door on me. Did I get the wrong person after all? Was all this for nothing? Then I replay his expression when I mentioned DUSSAL. He wasn't confused — he's lying.

"No, please! I've come a long way to meet you." I say quickly through the crack of the closing door. "I'm like you."

"Are you now?" Trevor holds the door slightly ajar. "It seems to me we're nothing alike; I'm not annoying." The door proceeds to close again. As a last attempt I impulsively send a streak of flames through the crack. The door freezes in place for a moment and then opens again. I look behind at the main street to see if anyone saw me while shaking the smoke off my hands. Trevor looks me up and down, his eyes wide with wonder now. He looks past me into the main street and the surrounding houses, then pulls the door open fully. "Come in."

Trevor leads me into the living room.

"Can I offer you some tea?" he asks, as he wheels himself towards the kitchen.

"Yes, please."

He looks me over again and then continues into the kitchen. As I wait, I limp around the living room, my eyes sweeping over the space. The floor is carpeted, a single leather couch is paralleled by a couple of sofa chairs. A coffee table sits in between, topped with magazines. I find a cozy, but currently unlit fireplace against the back wall. I move towards the mantle. A framed picture shows what looks like a younger Trevor and a pretty woman. Perhaps his wife? The rest of the mantle displays several community awards. On either side of the mantle are shelves lined with books of all kinds, and more magazines. I spin slowly and notice half a dozen clocks placed all around the living space, all quietly ticking in unison. Trevor comes back with a tray on his knees. He puts it down on the table.

"You can sit." I lower myself onto the couch while Trevor pours tea into two mugs. I observe the snack tray: crackers, baby carrots, and a few sandwiches. My stomach growls deeply. Forgetting all reserve I have, I reach over and grab a handful of food and begin to wolf them down. "Slow down or you'll choke." I look up awkwardly and realize I'm being rude. I try to apologize but my mouth is still full of sandwich. I chew more slowly and swallow.

"Sorry," I say finally. "I'm really hungry."

"I can see that." Trevor sits back in his wheelchair across from me, his fingers politely and patiently interlocked. I wipe my mouth and pick up my cup of tea. "So what, they're recruiting teenagers now?" he asks.

"Recruiting?" I take a sip of the warm, sweet tea.

"Well, how did you get dragged into this?"

"My dad forced the drug on me — it's a long story."

"Your dad?"

"Yeah, James Craig."

"That son of a bitch is your father?"

"He's had this plan for my future with him at DUSSAL since I was a kid and had one of his agents trick my mom into taking the drug home to me. Then he had me kidnapped and brought to D.C. When I sneaked around one of the offices I saw your name in their files, I escaped and came to find you." I avert my gaze briefly, observing the mantle again. "I was hoping you could help me."

"Help you do what exactly? Trust me, they are not the type of people you want to mess with." Anxious to know what set Trevor apart from the other trial members, I jump to my next question.

"What happened to you? Everyone else in the files are deceased, but you survived."

Trevor chuckles darkly. "Barely. I barely survived. I knew there were others, but I was never told what happened to them. Guess the truth comes out eventually." I remain silent, waiting for him to continue. "You really want to know my story?"

"Yes."

Trevor slips into a moment of thoughtfulness, then he looks at my scraped leg and nods to it. "I saw you limping."

I look down at my torn pant leg. "Yeah. I-I got shot. I sealed the sound with my fire, but it still hurts." Trevor gestures for me to come closer. I hesitate, then slip forward.

"Let me see."

"Why?"

"You are a stubborn one aren't you? Roll up your jeans." Suddenly feeling awkward, I examine his face and try to determine his motive. What could he possibly do about my wound right now? Reluctantly, I do what he says. Trevor observes the red, scarred patch on my skin, then puts his hand on it and closes his eyes. I flinch. What is happening? A tingling and stinging sensation spreads over the wounded area. I feel my skin move and my nerves soften. Trevor removes his hand, revealing my leg, completely healed. I stare at it in disbelief, then look up at Trevor.

"Healing. That's your power?"

"Yes. But it's not nearly as much as I was able to do years ago," he replies as he leans back into his wheelchair.

"Tell me. What happened?"

Trevor pauses and exhales. He looks thoughtfully at the rug. "Fourteen years ago," he begins. "I had a wife, and a good job in business that paid well. On the side, I dedicated many hours to the community, donated to charity, organized events for school fundings, city clean ups. You name it, I wanted to be involved. But still I always felt like I wasn't doing enough, like I could be doing more to contribute to the world. My wife, of course, consistently rebuked my being away from home so often and how I never seemed to stop piling my plate on with more and more projects. I wouldn't listen.

Then one day I saw a flyer from this lab — DUSSAL — advertising their need for test subjects for a new treatment. "A military experiment for the betterment of humanity," it said. It was another opportunity to do something great, to really contribute to the advancement of my country, or technology, medicine. When I told my wife, that was the last straw for her. She said it was too risky, that I didn't even know what kind of treatment it was. She was afraid something might go wrong, and then what? She made me choose between her and DUSSAL, and I thought, how could I choose? I chose to go and told her I hoped she would be there when I came back.

When I got there, they told me that if the experiment succeeded I could be the first to join a new army force they were founding. How could I resist that kind of opportunity? Well, the drug kicked in after a day, and suddenly I had the ability to heal. They started bringing in wounded animals and people to test my abilities, to see how far I could take them. Day after day, the wounds I was tasked with healing got bigger and uglier. That's when things went wrong. By the end of the week, the drug started to backfire. They told me the energy I was expending to heal others was sapping the health out of my own body. I grew weaker. They ran some tests and told me at that rate I would be crippled within the next week. I was useless to them. They would send me home tomorrow. But not without signing a non-disclosure agreement. Their reputation was on the line, if they were to be the angel of the world, word couldn't get out that they'd kicked a cripple to the street.

I was so angry. After the way they treated me? There was no way I was going to sign that paper. So, they threatened me. They threatened to bring harm to my wife. That's when I realized I had gone too far. I signed the disclosure and they sent me on my way... Of course, my wife was gone when I returned. And I continued to deteriorate. A month later, my legs lost their function. Most of my ability faded as well. I sold my house and got the hell out of Washington. Now I only have enough power to heal small wounds." Trevor pauses for a moment, contemplating in silent regret. "I was foolish," he continues. "I let my pride and my obsession for greatness lead me to a place where now I can't even do half the things I could before."

I sit speechless before him. I had gotten so absorbed in his story it's like I almost forgot I existed. My body feels numb. I take a breath.

"I'm sorry all that happened to you," is all I can think of saying. I wish I could say something more meaningful but how do you respond to a tragedy like that? We sit in silence for a while, both staring into nowhere, the air hanging heavily in the room. Finally, I break the silence. "I don't know what to do next. I'm out of parents to go home to. I have no money. I can't hide, my dad will just find me again, and he won't stop looking. I'm the first one the drug has worked on successfully, he's not gonna give up. I was lucky to even get to you."

"You want my honest opinion, kid? Get as far away from them as you can. Leave the country."

"Where am I supposed to go?"

"I can buy you a one-way-ticket to the country of your choice. You go there and start fresh."

"Start fresh," I say under my breath. His generous offer surprises me, and getting away from all this crap sounds like a dream come true. But then I think of Caitlin. How could I leave her behind? She's the only person who has ever really cared about me. She's my best friend. My whole life seems to run through my head at super speed. I have always gone through my day to day just putting up with abuse and looking forward to a hopeful future. I think of how my dad left us. He hit a barrier in his marriage and when his few efforts to save it failed, he ran. He's a coward, and if I run I'll be just like him. I refuse to be anything like my father.

"No," I shake my head. "I think I need to fight back. I don't know how yet, but it feels like the right thing to do."

"Are you sure? We're talking powerful people here. You're one against a hundred."

"I have to do this. I want to fight back."

"You're a brave kid, I'll give you that."

"If you want to help me, though, I could use some money for a ride back to D.C. I spent everything I had left coming here."

Trevor thinks for a moment, a light shadow forming over his face. "I don't know if I could handle knowing I played a part of your getting yourself killed."

"Not to be rude, but you're not responsible for my actions. Whatever happens when I leave here is on me."

Trevor falls silence again, deep in thought. I sit anxiously, waiting for his decision. Without him, I am essentially out of options. If he refuses to help me, I'm stuck in Maryland with no efficient or quick way to get back to DUSSAL. Suddenly I feel exposed. This is one of the only times in my life where my future depends completely on one person, and I am being uncomfortably challenged to trust a total stranger. I suddenly notice I'm not breathing. I force myself to take in air slowly, not wanting Trevor to notice. Finally, he wheels over to a table and pulls his wallet out of a drawer. He flips it opens and pulls out a few bills. Wheeling back over, he hands me the money.

"Our world needs more people like you, Sam," he says. I smile. Hope floods back into my world, my nerves relax.

"Thank you, Trevor." My eyes travel around the room and then land on Trevor again. "I might need a few more supplies, if you don't mind."

"What kind of supplies?"

Chapter 12

I swing myself into the backseat of a taxi.

"DUSSAL Labs, Washington D.C." I say with confidence. The driver nods and pulls the car back onto the road. I try to rearrange my lumpy pocket so it sits comfortably at my side. Being a repair man, Trevor had several different kinds of aerosol cans lying around his workshop, and he spared one for me. A plan had begun to formulate in my mind as I talked with Trevor. Now, sitting in the backseat with time to think, I believe I have a solid plan. I just hope it works. Anything could go wrong; I could get caught and then crap would hit the fan. A vibration in my pocket makes me jump slightly. I pull out my phone, the screen displaying a silly picture of Caitlin in a wizard costume from last Halloween with her name above it.

"Caitlin?" I hold the phone to my ear and wait but no voice comes through. "Cait?" I try again. No answer. Concerned, I hang up and pocket my phone. What was that about? Bad connection? Did her phone die? Hopefully, if my plan works, when I've left DUSSAL behind again, I'll call Caitlin and see if she's okay.

A short amount of time later, I ask the taxi driver to drop me off a few streets down from DUSSAL. I hand him the cash provided by Trevor and step out onto the street. I walk to some backstreet and make my way over to the side of DUSSAL property, trying to stay out of sight as much as possible. A chain-link fence surrounds the entire facility. By now I also know that DUSSAL prides itself on its security system but is actually a little lacking in that area. Fewer guards secure this place than they make it seem, and from experience, whoever works in the camera room only pays attention about half the time. Although, they've probably fortified their security since my escape, which will make it difficult for me to sneak around like before. I sigh. Here it goes.

I arrive at the fence and crouch in the grass. A guard stands at the door of a side entrance, keeping watch. I stick my hand into my heavy pocket and pull out the aerosol can. Holding it, my eyes flick between the guard and the can. The thin metal heats up in my hand and I cringe, hoping it doesn't explode in my face. When I start to feel the pressure build up inside the can, I lob it over the fence as hard as I can. It lands meters away from the guard, slowly rolling to a stop. The guard looks at the can, wondering where it came from. At first, I think it didn't work, but then it explodes. I flinch and smile. The guard jumps back but quickly gets over his fright and approaches the can to analyze it. I use this distraction to execute the next step of my plan. I place my hands on my fence before me, curling my fingers through the links. Creating a blaze, the fence melts like butter, liquid chunks plopping into the ground below. I wait briefly for the metal to cool, then crawl through the jagged gap. I run as quietly as possible past the guard and around the back of the building, struggling to hold in a laugh. Too easy.

I spot a large generator installed against the back of the building, a couple fuel tanks sit beside it. "There you are," I say to the machine. There was no way I could have initially known it was here, but realistically a very sophisticated and modern-looking building like this would want to hide their ugly and bulky generator from general public view. I am glad to see I was right... my whole plan is founded on assumptions and luck. I place my hands flat on one of the fuel tanks and concentrate. The guard may be more alert now, which means I have to be more cautious. Come on, tank, heat up faster. I look at my surroundings. A few meters away there is also a large garbage dump. That will come in handy.

After what feels like a painfully long time, the metal becomes hot to the touch, which means it must be close to becoming a giant version of my initial aerosol can. I run to hide behind the garbage dump, again, cringing as I wait for an even bigger explosion to ring in my ears. My heart beats fast. Instinctively, I find myself curling into a ball.

BOOM!

The fuel tank explodes and begins to eat into the generator beside it. I hear the guard yell in the distance and risk a peak around the edge of the dumpster. The guard has approached the scene to inspect the damage... A second explosion follows as the second fuel tank catches fire. The guard stumbles back and fumbles for his radio. I withdraw my head.

"I need immediate back up! We have an explosion at the generator!" the guard shouts. I bite my nails as I wait. Footsteps on the gravel from the side exit make their way to the explosion site. I glance around the corner at my end of the building. No one seems to be coming out of the other exit door. My heart still thumping, I pull away from the dumpster. Gliding across the concrete wall, I reach the handle and curl my hand around it, watching it melt satisfyingly. I quickly wipe the liquid metal out of the way and stick my fingers into the hole where the handle was. I pull the door open and step inside.

Back within the white-washed walls, I sweep my surroundings cautiously and begin to navigate through the hallways. Focused on finding Dr. Wilson's office, I only just have time to twist myself into a connecting hallway as a guard hurries past. He doesn't notice my presence and keeps moving towards the back exit to join the others at the explosion site. My back pressed against the wall, I take a deep breath. I have to stay alert. I peak around the corner with careful urgency, then continue the other way. This way and that, I let my instincts guide me because my heart is beating too hard for my mind to lead the way.

Finally, I find the doctor's office. I try the door and it gives.

"Thank you, Clarence," I say under my breath. I slip into the office and go straight for the filing cabinet I know contains the files on past test subjects. There are only thirteen, mine included. Bingo — I reach in and grab the whole lot of it. Now all I have to do is get back out. I try to muster all the hope and positivity I can but my nerves are on fire with anxiety and fear of being caught. I need this to work, I want payback. I need the world to see what really happens here. Hands shaking, I secure the bundle under my arm and fly back to the door, checking that that the coast is clear, before slipping back out into the hall. Hurrying down the hall, I go as fast as my feet allow without making a sound.

"Property damage and theft."

I freeze. My heart drops heavily into my stomach almost painfully. I feel a shock go through my body. Suddenly I feel very hot. Blood rushes to my face.
"I hope this isn't becoming a pattern," James says. I turn around to look at my father, trying not to show him the defeat I already feel. Two guards bearing guns stand behind him. "Hand them over." I tighten my grip on the folders defiantly.

"No." A sharp pain spawns in my shoulder. I stumble, and just have time to notice the dart sticking out before my body goes numb. My limbs lose their strength and I drop the files. Darkness curls itself around the edges of my vision, and then I'm out.

My eyes slowly flutter open. I blink a few times, clearing the blur. I am back in the guest room. I try to move but, once again, my hands are tightly bundled into a cloth, tied around my wrists with rope. I struggle against it but the bind is too tight, cutting into my skin. I try to produce fire but nothing happens. I feel panic start to rise in my chest. No, don't go there. If I let claustrophobia take over it will be much worse for me. I breathe in through my nose and exhale through my mouth in repetition, forcing my mind to steer away from my tied hands. More than anything, I am furious. How could I actually believe for a second that I had a chance. I laugh angrily. Was it brave? Was it judgment clouded by determination? Or was it just plain stupid? But then, would Trevor have really made up his mind to help me if he didn't think I actually had a chance? I wonder what will happen next. With security tighter than ever, and the whole complex expecting fight-back, now I have nothing going for me. I'm just going to be prisoner to my father, to this freakin' white cell of a building, and slave to an army I don't believe in. I stand up abruptly with a spur of energy. I refuse to accept that this is my life.

I look at the clock on the wall, it's evening. Just now do I notice a tray on the table containing a plate of food and a plastic fork placed neatly beside it as if to mock me. I look at my bundled hands.

"Is this a joke?" I mutter. With a sigh, I sit at the table, lean over the plate and begin to eat with my face. I wipe my mouth on the cloth around my hands, and consider smashing the plate, but I decide that destruction will only contradict my desire to remain calm and composed.

I stretch the leftover sleep out of my muscles and sit on the edge of the bed. A couple of hours pass... I'm sure I won't be able to sleep tonight. I pace the room hoping it will help me forget my boredom and rising feelings of frustration. I kick at the walls idly and swing myself around the room. Finally, I settle down on the bed again. Despite my restlessness, I know I will need as much energy as I can get for whatever happens tomorrow, so I lie down and close my eyes.

I wake up to the sound of knocking. I open my eyes and they are immediately drawn to the bar of light shining underneath the door. I turn to the clock. So I managed to sleep through the night. Although I don't feel too rested, I know it'll be enough. The door opens and a guard walks in with a tray of breakfast. I pull myself up and off the bed, stiff from sleeping with my hands tied together. My arms and neck ache. I watch as he swaps the new tray for the old one.

"When will I be allowed to leave my room?"

"When Mr. Craig says so," answers the guard, carrying the old tray.

"I can't stay in here forever!" The guard opens the door.

"Complaining will make it feel longer." The guard locks the door behind him. I walk over and stare at it for a while, as if doing so would make it magically unlock for me. I lean my forehead against the wood and close my eyes. When Mr. Craig says so. I wonder how long it will take for my patience to run out. I twist my body around to face that darn clock with my head still leaning against the door. A watched pot never boils, they say. More than ever I wish that weren't true.

Chapter 13

My plate of food has been empty for hours now, save a couple of salad leaves, and here I sit on the edge of my bed in extreme boredom. All I've been able to do is sit and pace and think since last night. My inactivity has drained energy out of my body, and now all I can do is sit lazily on the bed and hope someone comes for me soon.

A clicking sound makes me turn my head. The door opens and I jump to my feet, suddenly full of energy again.

"It's time to go."

I follow the guard down the hallway in silence, the sound of our footsteps echoing off the concrete floors. I break the silence.

"Where are we going?" As per usual in this place, I get no answer. We finally arrive at the gymnasium. More tests? The guard opens the door to let me in and I step through into the large rubber-floored room. I double-take — what I see sends a chill down my spine. Caitlin is tied to a chair with James standing on one side and a guard on the other.

"Caitlin," I choke. At first, Caitlin doesn't move or even look up, her eyes fixed blankly on the floor. I swivel over in the direction of the observation room, glaring at the scientists sitting behind their glass shield. "What did you do to her?" I say, turning on James. He steps forward.

"It's been quite an eventful twenty-four hours for your friend here. We gave her a dose of Wild Rose, and I must say I am very pleased with the results. Surprised, actually, at how well it settled. And I can assure you, she's nothing like the Caitlin you know. A few tweaks here and there, and now she suits our immediate needs. Caitlin, say hello to Sam."

Caitlin lifts her head slowly, her eyes landing on mine. What I see is pure hatred. Goose bumps form on my arms. The hairs on the back of my neck stand straight.

"What did you do?"

"I, personally, didn't do anything," retorts James.

"You're an asshole."

"I'd watch my language if I were you." I stare at him, anger bubbling within. He sighs. "Look, Sam. We need you, that's the truth. I've waited too long, worked too hard on this project to take no for an answer, you have to get that. You are vital to the future of DUSSAL. So here's the deal. You sign our enlistment contract, pledging yourself to DUSSAL's future army, and we let Caitlin go. Don't sign the contract and you can say bye to your friend."

"You went too far!" Water rises to blur my vision.

"And I could go much further, trust me, Sam. Power is a fruitful tool."

"How do I know you're not lying to me again?"

"That's a risk you're going to have to take." I look at Caitlin again, her slumped posture, hair hanging messily around her face. Her bloodshot eyes, still fixated on me in a rock-solid stare of hatred. I shiver.

"Will you undo what you did to her, if I sign the papers?"

"It will take time, but if that's your only request, it's a small favour in exchange for a lifetime of service."

Every bit of me repels the idea of trusting James. After everything he has done, the way he seems to have no problem in ruining my life, like everything I care for doesn't really matter, how could I trust him? But a larger part of me would willingly throw it all away to free Caitlin. Her future looks more promising than mine. She knows where she's going, she has a family. And even though she'll have this obstacle to overcome, I know she's

122

strong and she'll be able to move on. Most importantly, she's the only person I truly cherish, the only one who has stuck by my side my whole life.

"Okay, I'll do it," I say. James gestures to the guard on Caitlin's other side and he brings forward a folder. He places it on a table in a corner of the room which I just notice. I walk over slowly, then the guard unbinds me and hands me a pen. I lean over the table and, after skimming them briefly, sign the documents. I drop the pen and turn to face James. "Right. Your turn."

"I don't think so." My heart drops into my stomach.

"I did what you said!" I squeal. "She doesn't need to be dragged into this any further!"

"Sam," he answers casually, "You've caused a tremendous amount of damage to my property, you've put my project in jeopardy, and you've injured several of my men. It's only fair that we even this out. Besides, you need to be focused, and Caitlin is a distraction." James gestures to the same guard, who unties Caitlin. "Now I want you to show me that you're the warrior I know you to be."

Caitlin rises from her chair and approaches me slowly like I'm prey. I back up, intimidated by her demeanor. The most uncanny thing is that despite having known her my whole life, right now I don't recognize her at all. My skin tingles. Out of the corner of my eyes I perceive James and the guards retreat to the observation room, like they're getting ready to watch a show.

"Caitlin—" My voice is cut off when Caitlin's hand plants itself onto my throat. "Caitlin, it's me—" I choke. I struggle against her, hands clamped around hers, trying to pull them away. A cold sensation climbs up my neck. I attempt to suck in air but nothing passes through. Panic spreads through me, and I realize she won't stop until I'm dead. My hands heat up and steam against Caitlin's cold skin. Caitlin cries out and lets go, looking at her hands in anger. I move away, gasping and coughing. Caitlin yells and an ice ball flies in in my direction. I move out of the way, the ice ball crashing into the wall behind me. My eyes widen in shock. Caitlin forms another ball of ice, mist floating around her hands. Still trying to catch my breath, I move too slowly. The ball hits me in the shoulder. I cry out and stumble, eyes watering in pain. Clutching my shoulder, I stagger backwards. "Cait, please! I don't know what they did to you, but you need to wake up! I don't want to hurt you!"

"Too late! You already have," she says, her voice dripping with contempt. I open my mouth to answer but no words come out. This is a tone I have never known from my best friend. Caitlin extends her hand and sends a streak of ice towards me. Snapped to attention, I counter it with a streak of fire. Steam billows out of the middle where the two elements meet. The room quickly fills with fog. I blink away the growing numbness in my eyes. I stop my stream of flames and everything is quiet. The air in the room is opaque. Nervously I back up again. My gaze speeds around the space in alert, trying to locate any movement, each swift breath getting lost in the thickness of the air. Stupidly, I hold out a gently flaming hand as an attempt to see through the fog. A ball of ice shoots out from nowhere, propelling my arm backwards to the wall, firmly pinning in in place with a chunk of solid ice. I cry out, my hand already going numb, my arm burning in its socket. My hand glows within the ice and melts it almost instantly. I break free just to be frozen in place again with another lump of ice. Caitlin appears ominously out of the steam holding what looks like a spike of ice. For a second, I don't know what to do. I swallow.

Caitlin leaps onto me. Instinctively, I grab her arm with my free hand, holding the spike back. With my chest heaving, and my vision blurring again, I try to reason with her.

"Caitlin! I know you're in there. You like Greek mythology and comic books. Just the other day you were telling me about Centaurs. And you're the most caring person I know—"

"Shut up!" Caitlin wrenches her arm back and drives the spike down. I roll out of the way, my hand melting through the ice at the same time, sending me tumbling away as the spike crashes into the wall and shatters. I turn to face Caitlin, who throws ice at my feet. I am knocked to the ground, landing on my front. Aching, I flip myself over. Next thing I know, Caitlin is on top of me, a brand new spike of ice posed to strike. I lock eyes with her, hoping to draw out mercy, but all I find is an evil twinkle like she knows she's won the fight. Tears roll down the sides of my face.

"Caitlin, please," my voice cracks. "Try to remember." Caitlin's eyes linger blankly on mine in what feels like an eternal moment of suspense. I brace myself. Caitlin screams. Her hand comes down. At the same time, I scream, my hands bolting up to stop her arms above me. My hands steam against Caitlin's arms. A thick layer of ice spreads across her skin where it comes in contact with my clamping hands. I feel my strength draining. My arms tremble violently as Caitlin uses all of her force to push her weapon closer to my chest. With a final determined shout, I collect all of my strength into one last effort, and push upward. Caitlin's balled hands slam back into her face. She tumbles back, dropping the spike, and collapses limply onto the floor. Shaking and weak, I pull myself to my knees and crawl hurriedly over to Caitlin's still body. I place a hand on her head. A red gash shines on the bridge of her nose. More water pours down the front of my face. "I'm so sorry, Cait," I squeak.

"You did well, Sam." James' voice startles me. I had completely forgotten about him. The fight had closed Caitlin and I into a lonely bubble where nothing else existed. "You have a lot to learn, but that's what our training program is for." Suddenly full of energy again, I swing around onto my feet with a new fire burning in my chest.

"You're even more messed up than Mom was! Why did you have to do all this?"

"You weren't cooperating, Sam. You just needed a little push. This is your destiny." Annoyance flares up and adds to my anger. He doesn't even deserve to say my name anymore.

"No! Here I was trying to figure out what I wanted to do with my life, just to find out I never even had a choice!" I boldly march towards James, every part of me hot with anger and hatred. James glances quickly at his guards. "You're ruining my life!" I scream.

"I think you need some time to calm down. We'll talk again in the morning," James says patiently.

"No! No more talks! I'm done!" My entire vision is filled with flames. Frightened, I realize that my whole body is on fire. My hair, my skin, my clothes. A shout of panic escapes me. A guard steps forward with a small object in his hands. A sharp prick hits me in the side, then a wave of pain travels through me and I hobble to the floor. With my muscles tight, my body trembling, a tornado of emotions spinning inside me, I finally pass out.

Chapter 14

If my brain was groggy a moment ago when I was coming to, I am certainly awake now. I am thrown onto a cold, wet floor. Actually, wet is an understatement. The concrete floor is submerged in about six inches of water. I get up, splashing, and stagger over to the heavy metallic door which slams shut. I bang on the door with my fist.

"Let me out you—" My last word is drowned out by the sound of the door locking from the outside. The noise echoes in the room for a second, and then I am left in dark silence. I look around. What I am locked in is essentially what could be considered a water dungeon. The walls of this small room are thick and metallic. The door sits above the floor by half a foot, the water stopping almost level to the doorframe. I crane my neck. A camera is fixed into one of the top corners, its lens watching me closely. Right above me are sprinklers, set into the middle of the ceiling. I begin to feel claustrophobic almost immediately. I try to use my fire, but my hands, along with everything else, are soaked. I kick at the water furiously, screaming, then fall to my knees, breathing heavily. I fight an anxiety attack, feeling like I am about to burst with anger. I punch my fists down into the water over and over, sending it shooting up around me. And then I am still. I stare at my rippled reflection. It feels like I'm back to square one. No. This is worse than square one. At least before I still had a best friend who knew who I was, a kind of freedom I took for granted, and an independent life I was slowly, but surely coming to figure out for myself. I've never had much, but everything I did have has been cruelly and selfishly ripped away from me.

Tears roll down my cheeks, but I don't feel them. They drip down onto the water, continuing the rippling effect. I close my eyes. Voices echo through my mind. My mother's voice bouncing around my head calling me:

careless
ignorant
good for nothing

Some of her last words stab me again:

monster
ungrateful
lazy

James' words join into the jumble:

"I want you to join us."

"You belong with DUSSAL."

And out of the dark cloud of negativity, I hear Caitlin's voice:

"You're super smart, Sam."

"You'll figure it out, I know you will."

These final words reverberate through my mind. I open my eyes. The water is still now and I can see my reflection clearly. In the midst of chaos and misery, one thing has always proven true: my friendship with Caitlin. For the first time in forever peace spreads through my whole being. An abrupt sound sets off above my head and a shower of water rains down on me, drenching me again, but I remain still. The sprinklers stop. Suddenly I lift my eyes and straighten myself up, focusing my attention on the sprinklers. Under my breath, I begin to count the pause between sprinklings.

Moments later, I am surrounded, almost choked, with steam. Two minutes between sprinklings gave me time to focus all my energy on using my power. I learnt recently that I can produce fire with my whole body, and I used that. I couldn't produce fire, but I could produce heat. In raising my body temperature, I dried myself and increased the room temperature, evaporating six inches of water until only a puddle was left. Footsteps hurry down the hall and come to a halt. The door unlocks and opens. Steam filters out through the opening.

"What's going on in there?" a voice shouts from the hall. For once, I am the one to provide no answer. "Subject fourteen, answer us!" Limbs shaking in my hiding spot, I hope they don't leave me hanging too long. "We'll count to three and then we're coming in!" I grit my teeth. Two guards finally make their way inside. "It's dry!" the lead guard says. The two men look at the floor. The remaining water has seeped slowly into the concrete.

"Where is she?" asks the second guard. The first shakes his head.

"There's no way she could have escaped."

"Wait, what's that over there?" The two move towards the back wall. Now they see that parts of the wall have gashes where metal has been melted.

"What the...? Hey guys, come check this out." The second guard calls to more men standing in the hall. Two more enter the room to observe the melted metal. Grateful for relief from the strain in my arms, I let myself fall in front of the door and jump into the doorframe. The noise makes all four guards turn around in surprise.

"Have fun in there!" I say. I watch with a smirk on my face as everyone looks up to see the hand and footholds I melted in the corner above the door.

"Get her!" the leader shouts. I close the door on them before they can reach it and lock it. A sort of delighted evil laugh escapes my mouth and I run down the hall.

My moment of triumph lasts for but a moment. I try my best to remember how to weave in and out of the maze of hallways that will lead me to the lounge area. Sweating with anxiety and fear of what would happen if I were caught again, I finally break into the open space of couches and tall windows. The room is flipped. I frown, and then understand my feeling of disorientation. The water dungeon is found on the other side of the building from where my old guest room is situated.

The sun cuts across the floor and through the furniture in a line of warm gold. The giant clock on the wall confirms that it's late afternoon. Soon the sun will set fully, and then darkness will be on Caitlin and I's side as we try to escape. I make my way across the room to the other hallway opening and try to navigate back to the guest room. My gut tells me that's where she is, I just feel it. There's a sort of cruelty in my best friend being imprisoned in the same room as I was — the person she no longer remembers as her best friend. That kind of malice suits this place. I arrive at the guest room and try the handle. It's locked. I take a deep breath and melt the door handle. With my heart beating out of my chest, I open the door a crack and cautiously peak in. Through the gap I see Caitlin sitting on the bed, hugging her legs. Her eyes flick from side to side the way they do when she's deep in thought. She squints every now and then, which I know means she is going through a lot of confusion. I brave opening the door a bit more, knowing I don't have much time. I slip in cautiously, keeping my eyes on Caitlin like she's a predatory animal who can pounce at any moment, and close the door behind me. I swallow.

"Caitlin?" Caitlin doesn't move or speak. Her eyes steadily keeping their quick back-and-forth pace. I fiddle with my shirt, not knowing what to do with my hands. I feel like I'm talking to a stranger, but the face is familiar. The uncanny sensation gives me goose bumps. "Caitlin, we need to get out of here. Please." I lick my lips, my mouth very dry all of a sudden.

"We?" Caitlin responds without looking at me. "There stopped being a 'we' when you left me."

"I didn't leave you," I say, my eyes drifting awkwardly to the corner of the room. Suddenly, Caitlin's head turns so abruptly it startles me.

"Don't pretend like you don't know what happened. You betrayed me!" she says coldly.

"What are you talking about?" And then it dawns on me. A pure hatred that comes from seemingly fake memories. A disposition that doesn't belong to her. An inner struggle with confusion. They must have brainwashed her somehow. I push aside rising anger. I need to focus on getting her back. "Look, Cait, whatever you think happened, it's not real."

"Don't you dare gaslight me!" Caitlin stands up with a burst of furious energy and steps forward to face me. "I was in a really rough spot. The one time I really needed you, and you weren't there. And you knew about my fear. You knew I was afraid of being alone!" For a moment I am speechless, but I quickly snap myself out of it.

"Caitlin, I didn't know that about you — you never told me. I'm so sorry, I—"

"And then as if that wasn't enough, you had to go spread rumours about me to the whole school." Tears form in her eyes as she speaks. "Caitlin, you know what she doesn't in her free time? She plucks wings off flies, she tears legs off of grasshoppers, she catches mice in her backyard, she sneaks them into her shed where all the sharp tools are and—"

"Stop!" I shout, a sick feeling growing in my stomach.

"Not only did the school think I was a freak, but it also pretty much ruined my chance at becoming a vet. The one thing I was really certain about in life, and you ruined it. I never thought you capable of something like that." The tears that had built up in her eyes now fall down her face. A lump of emotion forms in my throat.

"That's because I'm not! I would never do these things to you!"

"And look! Now you've joined this army, which I find out is run by your dad, leaving everything behind including me, like you never cared about me in the first place." I groan in frustration and rub my face with my hands.

"I never said I would join him. I tried to escape! I only came back to try to take him down!"

"You have no right to try to justify anything! It's too late, our friendship is over." Tears now begin to flow down my own face.

"Caitlin, you mean more to me than anything. You're the only person I have. I'm not leaving without you! I don't care if you hate me. I will fight for you whether you like it or not." Caitlin angrily avoids my eyes. I sigh shakily. "Listen, I've always been afraid of failure, and it's prevented me from making important decisions in life. This whole situation is impossible. Getting out of here might be impossible, but I still came back because my best friend once told me that I would never know if I didn't try."

Caitlin stares at me blankly, almost like she is looking through me, like I'm just a wall. I plop myself down on the chair across from the bed, overcome by defeat. Caitlin stands still, fixed on the door before her. Suddenly, her gaze moves in my direction, her eyes flicker like her mind is fighting. I study her as her body turns to face me completely now. I stand, unsure what will happen next. She examines me intensely, her brows furrow, her lips pursed, and I wonder if she's about to pounce me again when —

She looks momentarily confused, like mental puzzles pieces clip and unclip in her mind. Her eyes drift and then blink before finding mine again, but this time I see they have found the spark that was missing before.

"Sam?" I stare at her tentatively, holding my breath. She furrows her brows again and then her eyes widen. "Sam!" I exhale in relief. We embrace. "I'm so sorry. I didn't want to hurt you. It felt so real. It still does..." She shivers.

"It's okay. I know you weren't yourself. I'm just glad you're okay." I watch her expression as it changes from grief, to anger, to great disturbance, her fake memories falling into her conscious. I put a hand on her arm.

"Hey, Cait. It's going to take some time. We'll work through it. I'm not expecting things to go right back to normal, but I want to help mend it." Caitlin smiles weakly and nods. "I love you," I assure her. Caitlin smiles a little more confidently, and then shakes her head as if trying to shake the memories away. I clear my throat. "Right. So now we kind of need an escape plan. We have little to no time, but we'll make it work. Any ideas?"

Chapter 15

Caitlin and I do our best to be as loud as possible, screaming and making crashing sounds from within the room. Hurried footsteps approach. Caitlin and I stand at the ready. The door swings open and the guard is welcomed with a ball of ice to the face. A second guard who was standing behind the first, moves out of the way as his colleague collapses unconsciously. He raises his taser and steps forward to see me stand in the middle of the room — but I'm only the distraction. Caitlin jumps into the doorframe from the side and kicks the guard in the groin making him fall back onto the floor, clutching his sore spot. Caitlin and I step over him into the hallway and I lean down to steal the unconscious guard's key card while the other is still disabled. We run, veering from one hallways to another in search of an exit, then we pass by Dr. Wilson's office. I slow down and backtrack.

"Sam! What are you doing?" Caitlin glances around nervously.

"We need to get the files!"

"What files? Do we have time?"

"It's important," I insist. "We can take down this whole operation. Back me up?" Caitlin looks unsure. Her eyes glancing anxiously down the hall again.

"Be quick."

I walk into the office easily and boldly.

"You really need to lock your door, Clarence," I say out loud. I go straight for the filing cabinet and open the second drawer... It's empty. "No!" I stand there for a second, wondering what to do.

135

"Um, Sam..." Caitlin's voice calls quietly from the hall, "We have company." I shut the drawer, frustrated, and turn back to the door. In the hallway, Caitlin's gaze immediately finds my empty hands.

"Where are the files?"

"They moved them."

"We need to go, now!"

"Okay, time for phase two. Ready?"

Eight guards appear at the other end of the hallway. Their black uniforms contrasting the white walls around them.

"There they are!" The guard in the front announces obviously. Caitlin and I don't stick around. The horde of guards chase us like hunters chasing foxes. Our eyes meet and we give each other a quick nod, then, as we go, I shoot fire at the walls while Caitlin shoots ice at every sprinklers she can. Her aim is much better than mine, when I think about our practice in her backyard forever ago. She gets most of them. The sprinklers remain plugged as the flames climb up the walls, painting a new coat of charcoal. We emerge into the lounge area. I look around frantically and remember the kitchen door. Kitchens always have access to the outdoors! I run towards the kitchen entrance and Caitlin follows.

"In here," I shout.

"What! Why?"

"Trust me." Caitlin looks nervous and uncertain but follows me into the kitchen. We duck behind a counter and continue to shuffle towards the back exit, panting and shaking. The oven beside me is the other reason that inspired me when I saw the kitchen. If I have time, I'm not parting without leaving a mark. I get to work with the oven, turning all the nobs to their max. We rise out of our crouching positions and reach for the door.

"Stop!"

Caitlin and I stop in our tracks and turn around slowly. James moves into the kitchen surrounded by the eight guards from earlier. He holds up the files I wanted. "Looking for these? You know, I always said you were a clever girl, but you're a bit predictable. This destruction has to stop." He says this calmly, but the vein popping in his neck tells me he has reached his limit. A subtle smile tugs at the corner of my mouth.

"That's too bad. I have more where that came from." James steps forward, standing just near enough to the oven. "I'm growing very impatient with you, Sam. I'm getting sick of your attitude. I promise to let your friend go right now if you stop all of this nonsense and honour the contract you signed."

"Sorry, I can't do that," I retort. I eye the oven anxiously. "And you know what? You're a lot like Gentleman Ghost."

"What are you talking about?" The impatience and strain grows in James' voice.

"Do you know what his weakness is? Nth metal." James nods to his guards, signaling them to grab Caitlin and I. The men in black approach, but I ignore them. "I'm your nth metal." As if on cue, the oven explodes. James and his guards scream as a wave of fire bursts out at them. Caitlin and I shrink back as the appliance's door flies off its hinges and the files are blown out of James' hands. I drop and crawl over to the files. Grabbing them, I quickly pat the flames off and run back to Caitlin. We open the exit door and step out into the fresh, cool evening air.

We don't stop. The two of us run for the parking lot gate.

"You said a nerdy thing! I'm so proud of you!" Caitlin shouts over the sound of the fire alarm in the background. For the first time in a while a smile has formed on Caitlin's face. I roll my eyes playfully and chuckle. Things would have almost felt normal again if we weren't still trying to escape an evil government organization. I glance over my shoulder. The guards have begun to pour out of the kitchen exit, beaten up and covered in soot. James stumbles out after them, coughing. The side of his left leg has a wet, red gash where he must have been hit by the oven door, and he is badly burnt. For a moment I feel bad because he is my father, but very soon after I remember everything he has done to me, and that, really, he is not my father.

"If you don't get them here this instant, you're all fired!" James' voice carries over the asphalt. I turn my eyes briefly again to see the guards rush forward. We are so close to the gate... Another eight meters, another six, another — My chest contracts and I begin to cough violently. No, not now. Not now!

"Sam! Hold on okay, I know you're struggling but we're almost there," Caitlin encourages. But I can't. I slow to a stop, gasping for air. Caitlin stops beside me. In the corners of my vision I see more guards than ever before filing out of side exits, probably their backups. I wonder if all the staff are here today, looks like they weren't taking any risks this time. A light glows behind me and I turn to see flames rising monstrously out of windows. Caitlin frowns and turns to face the opposition.

"Cait, what are you doing?" I say weakly.

"I think these guys want to go skating." Caitlin squats and touches the asphalt. Ice spreads from her hands out towards the running guards. It quickly overtakes them and forms under their feet. The men slip and fall on their backs, then try their best to get up but continue to slip ragingly. I laugh between coughs.

"Caitlin—" I say, short of breath. "That was—amazing!"

"Shout out to Elsa," she says. Caitlin helps me straighten up and keep moving. With her support we finish closing the distance to the gate. A woman in the gate control booth stands and yells at us. Caitlin throws a chunk of ice at the handle, locking her inside, and leaving her to curse and rattle the knob. We turn our attention to our last obstacle. The gate is locked.

"Got more Frozen in you?" I ask. Caitlin places a hand on the gate. Ice spreads quickly across the metal. Frost curls over the chain link, and the frigid metal shatters. The guards have managed to stand and begin sliding comically towards their vehicles. Caitlin helps me slip out of the hole in the gate and slowly we pick up a running pace again.

Further down the street, another explosion shakes the earth. Caitlin and I gawk at the flaming building, admiring our work. We perform an exhausted high five and don't stop until we are as far from that crumbling place as possible.

Chapter 16

Two weeks later, several news channels show images of a wrecked and scorched DUSSAL Labs. The anchors announce the shocking court case DUSSAL faces for the kidnapping of fifteen-year-old Samantha Grace and Caitlin Moore, and for the forceful use of unofficial drugs. It is also confirmed that DUSSAL is responsible for the death of eleven individuals. The facility has been shut down for further investigations over the course of the trials. Proud and satisfied with just being the one to have handed the files to the police, I gladly watch them do their work in taking down one of the evils in the world.

After escaping DUSSAL, Caitlin and I called her parents with the nearest phone we could find and explained what we could in a short amount of time. The distressed but relieved couple, who had just been in the works of putting up missing person signs for both Caitlin and I, booked a flight to meet us in Washington.

On getting back to Edmonton, the Moores' immediately began to look into the paperwork for legally letting me live with them. Once settled in, I contacted Trevor to let him know how things went. Although he knew how things had ended from the news, I gave him details on how my plan had unfolded. We keep in touch; recently he messaged me saying that I inspired him to hope again, and told me about this woman he had encountered and eventually befriended. He'd been developing feelings for her but hadn't been able to push away fear and find the courage to take the first step. Today, he's decided to finally pick up the phone and call her. I'm glad my story has been able to inspire someone and move them to action.

I guess at least I've done one thing right.

Apart from that, Caitlin and I have been attending therapy once a week. It's really helped Cailtin break down the lies that had been forced into her. I can tell she's coming back to her old self because yesterday she practically woke me up just to ask me if I would rather fight one horse-sized duck or a hundred duck-sized horses. As for my own therapy sessions, I have to say, little by little, I'm beginning to feel the weight of all my circumstances lighten.

Now Caitlin and I sit in the room we share, waiting to leave for school. Caitlin sits on her bed holding a notebook.

"So, it's a spoof on Robert Frost's Fire and Ice," she explains. She has been working on this poem she says is inspired by our new-found powers. Caitlin clears her throat. "Some say the world will end in fire/some say in ice/From what I've tasted or desire/ I hold with those who believe that fire and ice/ can come together and heal rather than destroy."

"That's beautiful," I say. "It doesn't rhyme though." Caitlin cranes her neck, half offended.

"Poetry doesn't have to rhyme."
I put my hands up defensively. "Hey, what do I know? I'm only the science girl, right?"
Caitlin smirks. "Apology accepted."

"Girls, you need to get ready to go!" Mrs. Moore calls from downstairs.

"We're coming!" Caitlin shouts back. We hop off our twin beds and assemble our last minute things. I grab my asthma pump and bottle of anxiety pills and put them in my pockets.

Caitlin and I hurry down the stairs and put on our coats and shoes. Mrs. Moore kisses Caitlin on the head, Cailtin smiles at her mom.

"You slept well?" Mrs. Moore asks her daughter.

142

"Yeah. Still have nightmares, but it's getting better." I know how she feels. We've both had nightmares since we got back. Sometimes we share them, sometimes it's too much to talk about. But we've never been more on the same level than now, when we've shared such a unique traumatic experience together. I don't feel like I'm the one who gets all the support anymore. Now we support each other.

"Okay. Are you sure I can't drive you guys?"

"Mom, we'll be fine. We're not going anywhere again."

"I know. I just still feel protective. My mama bear has re-emerged." Mrs. Moore pulls both Caitlin and I into a big bear hug. Caitlin rolls her eyes, smiling. I smile too and hug Mrs. Moore back. Caitlin and I grab our school bags off the floor and swing them over our shoulders as Mrs. Moore opens the door to let us out. "Have a great day, guys!"

"Thanks, Mrs. Moore," I say. We shuffle onto the front lawn and pull our bikes up to standing.

"And if you two aren't back by four I'm calling the police," Mrs. Moore calls out from the front door.

"Mom!" Caitlin laughs. We mount our bikes and push the pedals.

"I'm joking!"

"Bye!" Caitlin calls with a hand in the air, and we're off. Today, the sky is grey and the air a chilly, but it's nice because I get to share it with people who care about me. I feel like I am finally in the calm after the storm, like a whirlwind came and destroyed everything I hated about my life, swooping me up and dropping me where I wanted to be the whole time. With a family who loves me, in a home where I feel safe and comfortable. It makes every withering fall day feel like summer. Is that poetic or just cheesy? I guess I should stick to science. Caitlin single-hands her bike to point out a fat squirrel on the branch of a tree we're passing. It nibbles on an acorn, its tail curled up behind it, balancing its bulging sides. I feel like I can finally breathe. I can finally enjoy the simple things in life — like fat squirrels.

* * *

I sit at my desk in Careers class, examining the assignment before me. Caitlin sits a few desks across from me, already filling out her sheet.

"So, once you have filled in your top three career choices, you will be doing research on these, which you will include in your paper. In a week we will have presentations. If you have any questions—" I drown out the teacher's words and begin to write without much hesitation.

Police Officer
Lawyer
Social Worker

I glance over at Caitlin and notice that she was looking at me first. She smiles warmly and turns her attention back to her assignment. As soon as the bell rings I shove my stuff into my bag and follow the stream to the door. Caitlin and I walk down the beige hallways together, Justine waves at us on her way to her locker.
I turn to Caitlin, holding up a small stack of papers held together with a paper clip. "I'll see you outside."

I make my way to Miss Hicks' classroom. I knock on the door frame. Miss Hicks looks up for her desk and smiles.

"Sam! Come on in." I enter, papers in my hands.

"I'm done my story." I hand her the short story I had started and finished writing soon after I got back to Edmonton and settled in with the Moore's. Miss Hicks takes it and reads the cover page.

"Flaming Rose." Miss Hicks looks delighted. I smile shyly. "I wasn't expecting to get this so soon."

"Yeah, well, once I made a few changes, the rest of the story was easier to figure out. Turns out I just needed to give it a fresh start."

"That's great!" Miss Hicks grins. "Well, I'm really looking forward to reading it."

"Thanks," I smile back. "See you tomorrow.

"See you tomorrow, Sam."

I leave the classroom and sigh happily. When I step out into the bike rack lot, Caitlin is waiting for me by the door, looking relaxed.

"You gave it to her?" she asks.

"Yeah."

"What did she say?"

"She looks forward to reading it."

"I thought it was really good." I thank her with a smile, but it fades almost as quickly as it appeared. Caitlin sees the serious look grow on my face and tilts her head questioningly.

"You know, back at the lab, when you were... not you. You said something about your fear of being alone. Is that really true?"

Caitlin laughs nervously. "Yeah."

"You never told me."

"I didn't want to make a big deal of it. Besides you always had enough to deal with in your own life." My head drops slightly to the side, my lips parted in surprise.

"You're never a burden to me. I want you to feel like you can talk to me about anything."

"I know," Caitlin nods.

"Do you still feel that way?"

"No. No, I realized that I have nothing to be afraid of. I know I'm not alone." Consoled, a smile finds its place on my face again.

"Of course, you're not." We stand by the door still, in a comfortable moment of silence. "You know, I was thinking…" We begin to walk towards our usual spot. "If powers are real, there's a chance centaurs could be real too." Caitlin's eyes widen with excitement. She turns to look at me enthusiastically, her shiny straight hair swinging to the side.

"Yes! Wait, do you think they would be lab-grown, or would they live on some island nobody knows about?"

"I don't know. Island, maybe?"

"Maybe we should watch Narnia when we get home, give us some inspiration on this new theory. We could make a tent in our room and watch it in there on my laptop. With Twizzlers of course!"

"Man, we better make a stop at the grocery store on our way home, then."

"Good call. By the way, did you look into that book I suggested? I think it's very much your style. I know you're not much of a reader, but the character kind of resembles you, I think you would understand her, you know…?"

Caitlin continues her ramble, and I listen, glad that this is my life. Nothing more, nothing less.

Made in the USA
Monee, IL
21 October 2024

68445862R00085